My Week Without Gérard

a novel by Ivan Boris

My Week Without Gérard

A novel by Ivan Boris

First edition for general release published in the UK by Morbid Books, 2021.

All rights reserved.

Front cover image: 'A Friends' Reunion' (1922) by Max Ernst

Back cover image: 'Pietà or Revolution by Night' (1923) by Max Ernst

Graphic design by Karolina Grzelak

A list of works incorporated via the cut-up method is included in the credits on the assumption of fair dealing.

A CIP catalogue record for this book is available from the British library and in the Nielsen database.

978-1-9162640-1-4

www.morbidbooks.net

"Surrealism, as has been said, is not a school. It cannot be reduced to a style and does not even offer a unique way to feel: it opens a door onto all the unknown qualities of the mind!"

— Alain Jouffroy, *Lettre Rouge,* cited in *The Esoteric Secrets of Surrealism* by Patrick Lepetit (translated by Jon E Graham)

MONDAY

I

Lester Langway stepped off the train at Gare du Nord with the same naïve excitement that had always rushed through him when he came to the city of Inspector Maigret, Jean-Luc Godard and Françoise Hardy. Typically, it was extinguished with a blast of hot dread as soon as he stepped one metre outside the station to see the illegal taxi drivers ripping off tourists, homeless Arabs cradling addictions like puppies (and puppies like addictions), men in sports vests smoking and hustling, and the stench of piss in the stifling heat of June.

He turned and headed for the Métro, bought a book of ten tickets that he planned to make last the week. He hauled his bags onto the purple number 4 line southbound to Saint-Michel and emerged out of the wormhole with his fake Ray-Bans on, military shirtsleeves rolled up, a copy of a Gérard Derenne book under his arm. He had only started it on Friday, alongside panic reads of his newspaper columns from the previous year, a couple of long-form features about him in "quality" American magazines, and a few French articles, which were suspiciously light on details, noting his disappearance from public life.

One of the few Derenne books available to him in a British library, *The Ethics of Logic*, a work of "pure philosophy" from 1979, made no sense at all. In fact, none of the material Lester had read by Gérard Derenne seemed to justify his reputation in France as a "prophet," or the national "conscience." If anything, the impression Lester got from the clippings was that Gérard was a clown in an expensive suit and white scarf, a kind of circus philosopher suited more to the soundstage than the academy. "His clothes are precise but are his ideas?" one critic asked, while another philosopher called him a "crass booby," a parody of the French intellectual.

While this story would be of a primarily investigative nature, Lester also hoped to flex his intellectual muscles a little more than his editors had allowed in the past. So it was good to have done some background research, know a few of the key philosophical concepts, the lingo, the jargon, to enable himself to blend into the most refined social milieu he had ever encountered. Struggling to comprehend the concept of a superstar philosopher, Lester studied the cover, the image that was displayed on supermarket shelves. It did seem strange how a work of philosophy appeared to have been packaged more like an autobiography, with its photogenic author gazing at the viewer in a state of grace and poise like a member of the nobility, perhaps a mid-career rock musician—or maybe even a *Down N Out!* cover star.

Lester knew he had to stop thinking about fame and glory, else they would never arrive. There were more immediate concerns, such as where he would sleep that night. He bundled into the famous bookshop, swarming with American tour parties in the location Hemingway was said to have perused the shelves. He approached the sales assistant. "Excuse me," swiping his shades off.

"Yes," stamping a book for another customer, the bespectacled man spoke English.

"You allow travelling writers to sleep here?"

"Yes."

"I write for *Down N Out!* magazine. I think I have a place to stay, but if that doesn't work out, can I crash here?"

"We're full until Thursday. Come back then and speak to the owner."

That wasn't much use if he was homeless tonight. Who were they allowing to sleep here, anyway? By the looks of it, middle-class American backpackers who could afford a hotel.

A security guard kept watch over him as he navigated the crowded crannies, perspiring like a shoplifter. To even reach the shelves where a recent work of personal essay or literary journalism by Gérard Derenne or his closest ally Jacques Dutronc might be housed would be impossible, and might just give him an anxiety attack.

Lester was standing outside checking his phone, charged on the Eurostar, when he looked up and saw a blizzard of grey hair going past him. "Professor!" he said, touching the elbow of his black suit. "I'm Lester Langway, *Down N Out!*, thank you for coming to meet me here." He flashed him his press card, but the philosopher wasn't impressed.

"Horrible," Jacques Dutronc said. "It is horrible here." He was just as grumpy as he appeared in the trailer for *Gérard & Jacques*, the sentimental buddy movie about the pair's forty-year friendship. It was the most recent and least badly received of Gérard's three attempts at directing films. "Why don't we go back to my office?"

"I'm sorry, I don't think I could make it all the way to the Sorbonne with these bags. Besides, I wanted to come and buy a copy of your book."

"Which one?" The philosophy don squinted in the sunlight, clearly testing him.

"*Sex, Lies, and the Moral Law: A Kantian Critique of Seduction.*" Lester tasted his cheek with his tongue. He knew he'd dropped a clanger.

"We are having some legal problems." Dutronc must have been referring to the plagiarism court case that had seen the book, published by Editions Derenne, pulped, and the publisher liquidated.

"What is it you want to talk about? I have a postgraduate seminar in half an hour."

"Well," Lester breathed out, "to cut to the chase, I'm looking for Gérard. I want to know why he's disappeared from public life—why he no longer writes his columns, appears on TV, even on mastheads. Did he quit, or was he dropped?"

"Alright," infusing his contempt with a silent *rosbif*, "but *why* are *you* looking for Gérard in Paris? He left the city six months ago and has no plans to return."

The instincts of the world's most renowned expert on Immanuel Kant cut through him. "Because it's my job."

"And what is your job exactly? I mean, what is it your write about? Can I have a look at one of your books?"

"I'm still working on my first book," he exaggerated. "This story might make it in."

"Interesting, and who is your publisher?"

"I'm on a freelance retainer with *Down N Out!* media, an

independent..." fumbling in his bag, hoping he remembered to pick up the back copies from the office this morning... "an independent publisher of quality journalism, reportage, cultural criticism and, uh, photography. Here you go," flipping the pages, "that's my by-line there."

"Hmm." Dutronc gave the impression that he would normally wear protective gloves to handle such material, turning the glossy pages at the corners with his thumb and forefinger as though they were smeared with something unpleasant. " 'Smoking Crack with Manchester's Young Tories.' "

"Hmm, yes, like I say..."

"Very sensationalist, very superlative, very..." Dutronc skimmed the first column of text. "I did not know that crack was so cheap in Manchester. Did you really smoke it?"

What was the right answer to that question? To any question? He remembered the moral imperative. "Only for research purposes."

"You are a committed professional then, Mr Langway." Dutronc's eyes popped when he saw the full-page photo of the young Conservative chugging on a crack pipe Lester had snapped in a hotel room at the conference. "What happened to this young fiend?"

Hardly Lester's proudest moment, it was still his most lucrative, having sold the images for ten times the amount he received for the eventual *Down N Out!* feature. "He was thrown out of the Tory party, then he attempted suicide. Now I think he works in PR." He realised now that this was the worst article he could have shown, as it looked like he was planning a hit piece. "Look in the other issue. I wrote a very sympathetic profile of the snooker player Ronnie O'Sullivan."

"Hmm," Dutronc flipped through the pages dismissively. "You know, while writing his book about them in the eighties, Gérard smoked opium with the Mujahadeen?"

"I did not know that."

"Well, there you go. Not quite such a professional after all?"

Dutronc handed the magazines back. The young reporter hadn't expected an intellectual titan to be so droll. He wanted to take the man to a bar and get him drunk. When he slid his phone out of his pocket it told him that he only had ten minutes left with Gérard's closest friend and confidante. "I was reading Gérard's last newspaper column from December, seeing if I could find any hints of a farewell..."

"You know how he wrote that column?"

"No."

"While he was having a shit."

"Oh."

"He has Dictaphones in every bathroom and at each end of his swimming pool."

"Really? I often have my best ideas while... nevermind." Lester had his notebook out, and was leafing back to the pages he'd scribbled while in front of his laptop. "When he wrote, 'I am taking a break from these pages for a while, and I do not know when, or if, I will return. But remember, I will always be in your sacred heart, Paris,' is that a reference to the Sacré-Cœur, the Church of the Sacred Heart?"

"That would be a literal interpretation," Dutronc smiled. "But remember, Gérard was not just a philosopher, a journalist, a television star, a businessman, a philanthropist. He is also a magician, a mystic, a magus."

"Of course... Do you think I could speak with him? We could arrange a very sympathetic interview. I can't give copy approval, but I would be happy to submit some of the questions in advance."

"No, no, no, it doesn't work like that." Dutronc chuckled at the novitiate's effrontery. "To speak with Gérard, there are procedures in place. One must meet certain standards. So if you please. Come, follow me."

II

Outside Cluny—La Sorbonne Métro they came to a police roadblock. Cops in shorts and sunglasses stood with their hands on their hips like in a Tom of Finland cartoon. Some were on rollerskates, others had machine guns—a very confusing message to be sending out. Parisians, irate at the state's foot patrolmen, were gesticulating and spitting on the pavement, questioning the reason of it all, but it made no difference, they would have to go the long way around. The professor snarled at one of the policemen blocking the road to campus, and they simply waved him and Lester through, as though being a philosopher—or perhaps, one of Gérard's men—gave you the keys to Paris.

They entered through the gates to the Observatory of the Sorbonne. It was the end of term. Students were draped on the edge of the fountain with a sense of confidence and style that Lester hoped he shared, or even surpassed, having obtained not just a bachelor's degree but a postgraduate diploma in Journalism. "Let me ask you a question." The professor gruffly nodded his head at students who greeted him in the corridors. "You must have an opinion on what is happening in France at present with the protests, the civil unrest."

Lester tried to remain indifferent to the eyeballs trained his way, as though he might appear as a guest lecturer being shown around. "I believe that as a journalist, it is my job to be impartial. To *understand without judging*, as one of your finest authors, Georges Simenon said."

If he made a good impression during the interview, he wondered if he might wrangle a teaching gig at the Sorbonne. Images of a lush apartment and a lecture hall full of fawning students flashed through his mind.

"Alright, and what is your *understanding* of the situation, Mr Langway?"

He ought to have researched the political upheavals before coming, and made a note to read the press every day. "I was going to ask you, are the protests really about wearing Speedo's in public pools, or are they a revolt against globalisation?"

Dutronc didn't respond. They had reached his office. A proper office, unlike that *Down N Out!* cowshed. Rows of mahogany bookshelves were lined with leather hardbacks. A gold-framed painting of his beloved Kant was hung behind Dutronc's huge regency desk. Facing it was an equally massive portrait of Gérard in a black, personally tailored Berluti suit with the trademark white scarf tossed over his shoulder, enhancing his golden equine features. Helmut Newton had taken it for *Vogue* in the nineties, when Gérard's hair was still dark. As his university friend Mushroom Daley used to say about the long-haired kids on campus, if Gérard was a bar of chocolate, he would lick himself. Lester couldn't help but see him aged by twenty years, the *Down N Out!* masthead pasted over the top and his own name on the cover.

"Sit down." Dutronc motioned to a comfy chair, surrounded by heaps of books on the floor. "And before I forget, please take a book from the pile by your feet. I need to clear some room."

Lester selected a hardback off the top of the pile and slid it onto the desk, hoping he could conveniently forget it. "You said you have a seminar? Aren't I..."

Dutronc smiled condescendingly, poured a glass of water from a tumbler and offered it. So this was the postgraduate seminar... Lester took it, wishing it was gin.

"You know, your work," and here came the appraisal, "your style, your whole manner of being is very awkward, Mr Langway. Would you like another glass of water? Or perhaps something stronger. You look a little hot and bothered, and how should I say, nervous?"

"Gin," Lester burped, covered his mouth. It would be breaking his new rule against drinking on the job, but he knew he would feel calmer and his hands would stop shaking. "I mean, yes please."

"Where did you study?"

"University of the East Midlands. An art college, really."

"And what did you read?"

"Political Science."

"And yet you know nothing about politics! I must say, you remind me of that American fellow, Hunter, what was his name?"

"Hunter S Thompson."

"That's right, like Hunter Thompson without any of the political insights. Would you like another drink?"

"Go on, then."

"Gérard doesn't like gonzos, is that what you call them?"

"It's not an official genre."

"Is it not?"

"I don't know anyone who would call themselves a gonzo. It's a bit naff."

"Gérard is an essayist in the grand tradition. His book about America is as perceptive as de Tocqueville. His rhetoric is on a par with Mencken, and he has the conscience of Zola. He is a guardian of language and culture."

"I wouldn't say I'm quite on a par with Mencken or Zola yet, but I have read them, and I agree, they have a certain grace that some of the contemporary stylists lack. I have my own style, my own..."

"Perhaps you are just an amateur. A fool. Have you considered that?"

"I beg your pardon?" Anxiety levels going through the roof, Lester fumbled through his tatty wire-bound notepad for a question to ask, but he was lost in a flurry of thoughts. "Hold on just a minute. Here we go. I have prepared some questions."

But Dutronc cut him off. He squinted as if into stage lights. "Everything tends to make us believe that there exists a certain point of the mind at which life and death, the real and the imagined, past and future, the communicable and incommunicable, high and low, cease to be perceived as contradictions."

The ice clanked against Lester's teeth, and it was as if his mind had frozen. "I think I get what you mean." He held his glass out for another one when Dutronc got up to signify their time was up. He chuckled to himself as he took the glass from Lester with one hand and shook it with the other. "I can't grant you an interview. Have a nice time in Paris, Mr Langway."

Lester was too shell-shocked to say anything. Trudging down the long corridor, he realised that he had made a terrible mistake coming to Paris, and wanted to go to the nearest internet café to book a return trip home. He was almost at the front desk, about to go through the metal detector, when he heard a voice calling him.

"Mr Langway!" It was Dutronc, chasing him down the corridor in his slippers. He handed Lester the book he'd forgotten to take—a huge, hefty volume that wouldn't fit in his bag, and he would struggle to carry. "I recommend you read it carefully. You never know what—or who—you might find between the pages."

With a shrug of the shoulders, Dutronc was gone.

Outside in the sunshine, Lester inspected the spine, expecting a dry philosophical text, but was pleasantly surprised by what he'd come away with: *Revolution of the Mind*, a 700-page biography of the Surrealist poet André Breton. He had read *Nadja* on the recommendation of Mushroom Daley, and not been terribly impressed by the overlong sentences and lack of plot. He couldn't understand what his friend, who was destined for the military academy, had loved so much about the whimsical love story. The *Manifestoes of Surrealism* he remembered a little better, and preferred their acerbities. He sat on the edge of the fountain in the courtyard to cool off and figure out whether to stay or go.

III

It was only 3pm and Lester needed a shower as well as a place to sleep. He had checked his phone, but there were no affordable trains back to London in the next seven days and the bus would be unbearable in this heat. None of Gérard's editors or publishers had replied to his messages. It was not surprising if he really did radiate amateurism and foolishness even in text format. He'd had his chance with his subject's closest ally, and he'd blown it.

Whether he liked it or not, he was here for what now seemed like an interminable tunnel of time. Seven days, a hundred and sixty-eight hours. Put it like that, and it didn't seem so long at all. How many hours did Woodward and Bernstein bill for Watergate? A hundred times as many, with ten-thousand times the resources.

Although what was it Dutronc had said about past and future ceasing to be contradictions? Would he really have chased Lester down a corridor in his slippers to give him something if he wasn't trying to tell him something? Leafing through the Breton biography, he noticed a location circled in red pen:
THE BUREAU OF SURREALIST RESEARCH
15 Rue de Grenelle

It was only a short walk across the Jardin du Luxembourg, so what the hell, he might as well go over and see what was happening. If nothing else, it was a piece of the city's literary history he had yet to sample. According to the biography:

> The Bureau of Surrealist Research opened its doors on the afternoon of Friday, October 10, 1924 (the Bureau register mistakenly says Friday the 11th) at 15 Rue de Grenelle, on the ground floor of a large private villa with concave façade called the Hotel de Bérulle. The space, which was rented by Pierre Naville's father and offered to his son's friends the way future fathers would donate garages to fledgling rock bands, stood in the heart of a district generally known for its staid ministries and sumptuous *haut-bourgeois* apartments.

Lester approached the grand entrance to the villa with a can of his favourite beer, Desperado's, cooling his palm. He rubbed it along his forehead and cheeks, absorbing its cool glow into his skin, whose pores were leaking grease. He put the can on the ground so that he could clutch the bars of the building that guarded the windows to try and peek inside. What rationale could he concoct for going in? He took one final swig of beer, then rang the intercom.

The door clicked open. In the darkness, he pawed around like a blind man until he found a handle and gave the big hulk of wood a shove with his shoulder. He bundled into the big reception area. With its thick red carpet and high marble ceilings, its walls tapestried in deep red, only a couple of art deco lamps emitting sepia glow, it was like stepping into another era. There was no doubt it had a delitescent power. At the reception desk two women in contemporary office suits with military epaulets, one of whom wore an eyepatch, were working at computer terminals disguised as 1920s Smith-Corona typewriters. They leapt up and eyed him suspiciously.

"We're not open to the public. Do you have an appointment?"

"My name is Owen Appletree," he said, getting his notebook out. "I'm an architectural researcher making a survey of the buildings occupied by the Surrealists."

"No photos," the woman in the eyepatch hissed.

"Who are you, a Surrealist?"

"No, but it says here," reading from Mark Polizzotti's biography of the Surrealist poet he had open on his knee: " 'Breton intended the Bureau, which was also called the Surrealist Central, to be a centre of contact and information for interested individuals. As one press release specified: "The Bureau is devoted to collecting by every appropriate means communications relating to the various forms that the mind's unconscious activity is likely to take." All interested members of the public were invited to come and display their subconscious wares between the hours of 4.30 and 6pm, Monday through Saturday. On the seventh day, Surrealism rested.' It's just gone 4.30 on Monday. I wondered if I could come in for five minutes and take some notes."

"Five minutes? Write down anything you see here on the ground floor, but access to the upper levels is strictly forbidden."

"Gotcha."

"And no photos!"

"Alright, alright," backing away, "no photos, I heard you the first time."

Lester guessed that the Surrealist Central now belonged to some kind of kooky burlesque theatre company with a paranoid director. At the entrance to marble stairway there was a metal detector he dare not approach, let alone walk through. The woman in the eyepatch gave the impression that she knew karate. On the walls, in ebony frames, hung what appeared to be original paintings by the symbolist painter Gustave Moreau. A man in a bowler hat was sitting stooped over a grand piano, while another he had failed to notice from the outside was peering through the thick red floor-to-ceiling curtains. On closer inspection, they were dummies, dressed in 1920s period costume. Lester could feel an eyeball trained on him as he examined the fat man at the Joanna, whose finger tapped on the lid and he emitted a coughing sound. The reporter jumped back amazed. He wanted to stay in this cool, dark enclave of antiquity, but his time was almost up.

"For my survey, I just need to know, who occupies the building post-Surrealism?"

"This is the office of ESCHATON Productions."

"Oh, what do you produce?"

"Paperwork."

"And your name is Owen Appletree? Stand here and have your photo taken."

"I thought you said no photos."

"You're not allowed to photograph us, but we are *obliged* to photograph you."

"Um, I'd sooner not, if that's okay?"

"Look straight ahead into the camera." The woman shoved a lens on a stick in his face. He tried not to look embarrassed. The other one slid a guest book towards him. "Name, date, signature."

The door behind him appeared to be locked. There was no way

out of this. Dithering, he noticed that there were two guest books—one for visitors, another for staff. He scribbled something illegible in the visitor book and wafted himself with his notepad, trying to keep up a casual appearance. "Do you happen to know of anything happening tonight? Any interesting buildings that are open? Parties that might be going on?"

The women glared at him.

Opening the door to the outside world was like stepping into a Belle Époque oven. Adjusting his eyes to the brightness, he slid his phone out of his shorts and began looking at his messages. His Parisian friend Freddy had finally replied, offering him the couch to sleep on. He pecked at the screen, sincerely thankful, and called the only person in his class to pass the shorthand exam.

"Hello, Western Rural News, Tom Perkins."

"Hello Mr Perkins," Lester said in a Welsh accent. "I've got some information about those missing sheep."

"What you doing in Paris? Some hot new baking trend?"

"Speak up, I can't hear you," Lester screamed with his finger in his ear. "There's some cunt drilling nearby."

"What do you want, Les? I'm busy."

"A quick database search."

"It'll cost you ten quid."

"Fuck off." Lester scared an old lady. "Sorry, madame."

"What do you want to know?"

"Do you have access to French company databases?"

"Why would a Welsh news agency have access to French company databases?"

"You know how these things work. I want you to go onto their version of Companies House and send me the shareholders and any other information associated with ESCHATON Productions."

"ESCHATON Productions, anything else?"

"Yeah, see if you can pull an address for Gérard Derenne."

"The philosopher?"

"The wanker."

"Okey doke. Do you need anything else?"

"Yes," Lester looked down at his feet in panic. "I've walked into some fast-drying concrete. It looks like I really am stuck here. The address is 15 Rue de..."

Perkins clicked off. It was sure to be a good one for the pub later.

IV

At 5.15pm, Anaïs bounded down the street in her bloojeans and filthy Converse sneakers, camera swinging on a lanyard, laughing at the English asshole and his latest escapades. Even though there was no breeze, her tangled dark hair blew across her face, which was pale and strangely concave, emphasising her jawline and her cheekbones.

"Can you believe it?" Lester announced, flapping his arms in disbelief. She leaned in to give him a kiss on the cheek. "I wouldn't come any nearer if I were you."

"Seriously, how the hell did you do this?"

"I wasn't paying attention."

"Oh, Lester, you never pay attention."

"I need you to get me out of here in the least humiliating, least time-consuming and least expensive way possible."

She counted on her fingers. "You can't have them all. Choose two."

Already humiliated, he'd take the cheapest, fastest way out.

Anaïs dialled a number. "Hello, there is a *rosbif* in the 6th Arrondisement who got himself stuck in cement. I don't know what he was thinking either. Three hundred Euros for being such an idiot? Alright, he says that's fine, he will pay it."

Lester was motioning "no, no, no," but then she showed him the homescreen on her phone. There was no fire brigade. "Just take your shoes off, you idiot."

There was something about walking through the streets of Paris with a pretty girl that made Lester feel like he was in the clouds. Even in socked feet, with cigarette butts sticking and stones stabbing at his soles, the place took on a magical potency that it lacked when wandering alone. Halfway down the street, he and Anaïs stopped to look back at the pair of desert boots in the concrete, and he pointed out how it resembled a Surrealist painting by Magritte. Skipping down the Boulevard Raspail, they sang the song, 'Le Feutre Taupé' by Charles Aznavour: "Drinking café frappés (with straws) / on the

My Week Without Gérard

Boulevard Raspail..." One of the many things he loved about this old French music was the frivolity, the unashamed confidence of a song about looking cool and drinking coffee. They stopped at a café when Lester's feet began to hurt. "It doesn't matter where you go, they're all as bad as each other," Anaïs assured him, taking a seat on the crowded terrace.

"So how are you?" she asked, rolling a cigarette from a little pouch.

"Pretty good." He grabbed the tobacco and assembled one, hands barely shaking now. When the waiter came along, his aspiration to be like Charles Aznavour fell by the wayside, as he couldn't help but have himself a beer, just a small one before switching to frappés. "A little stressed about this job."

"You don't say. Gérard is the most famous man in France. Why are you trying to interview him?"

"It's complicated." Lester flicked his ash on the floor.

"Is this for *Down N Out!*"

"Yeah, kind of, although I was also thinking it might form the basis of a book, if all goes to plan."

"A book?" Anaïs was obviously impressed and somewhat dumbfounded by his confidence. "Where will it start, at your birth, or with you coming to Paris?"

"Here, you can have a look at the first few pages if you like. It might explain a few things."

Lester gave her the black notebook that he'd bought especially for this assignment. He'd filled the first few pages on the Eurostar. Pretty much his only loyal reader, Anaïs seemed genuinely excited to be given a first glance.

PROLOGUE

I was late getting to the magazine office on Old Street, having been up until midnight drinking in the Ivy House. When the pretty young receptionist dressed in all black pointed to my shorts and yellow windbreaker and asked me what "patrol" I was on, she must have either confused me for a boy scout or suspected I was blagging access to the bathroom. "You're a vendor?"

I was hardly unused to being confused for one of the magazine's homeless street salesmen, but this was the first time I'd had it from one of the staff.

"I'm here to collect some back copies," I told her.

"What back copies?"

I took an exasperated look around the office, a former Fort Knox of fashion. On the exposed red brick walls, blown-up cover stars loomed beneath the legendary white masthead: Beyonce, Eminem, The Strokes, Tony Blair. Boxes of clothing samples, records and binders were packed and ready for the removal van. Most of the desks, knocked-up out of old toilet doors, had been cleared, and there were no staffers in besides this bimbo on desk duty, even at 10.30am. "This is still the *Down N Out!* office, isn't it?" Having written for this sinking ship for a year, I was no longer amazed that such an imbecile could land a staff job while there were ten thousand unemployed graduates in Hackney alone—or as I call myself, *freelance*.

"It is, at least for the next two days."

"I'm going to miss my train to Paris. Tim wanted to see me."

"Oh, I used to live in the Marais. Are you going for Fashion Week?" I was wearing my battered old desert boots... "That was a joke, obviously," she sniped. "Are you here to help with the removal?"

She obviously hadn't even read the magazine, where my features are becoming increasingly lengthy and serious.

"Take a seat and I'll let him know you're waiting, although he's currently in a meeting."

I sat down and chewed my nails, a poor substitute for breakfast, and reread Baudelaire's *Les Fleurs du Mal*. But there was a high-class woman's voice coming from the editor's private office. I strained to hear what they were saying, something about a model for the autumn issue, how if her parents wouldn't sign a piece of paper, Tim would have less than a fortnight to pull a cover star for the November issue out of his arse.

"Bye bye, lovely, have fun in Paris," Tim Sizebank growled to her in a deep, camp manner.

"Au revoir, Timmy, my handsome."

In her white cotton tights, Susan Twanky moved across the strip wooden floors like a heron down a bowling alley. The founder of Twanky Models' famous prosthetic leg was the most graceful and real thing about her.

My editor's bald head appeared. With his stripy tshirt and handlebar moustache, he looked like a gay prison scoundrel in a Genet novel. "If it isn't our star reporter," Sizebank said. "Come in, let's have a word."

My editor works in a replica of Arsène Wenger's office, and to get in you have to go through an original turnstile from the Highbury football ground. Much like the Arsenal manager, it is the consensus opinion in London media that he has lost much of his *va-va-voom* in the seventeen years since he co-founded the magazine. Still, he has always been good to me, letting me sleep in the office when my research requires it, or when I've been booted out of my house for stealing my housemates' drugs. As I was entering Tim's mancave, I got stuck between the floor-to-ceiling iron gates and suppressed a yell. Eventually fighting my way out, I emerged into the editor's office dizzy with a headache.

Barefoot, the editor leaned so far back in his flexi-chair he was almost upside down. He'd been up all night bookmarking apartments in Los Angeles on Airbnb. "Fancy earning a few extra quid? Is that why you're here?"

"Very funny."

"We need to be out of here by Wednesday morning."

I shuddered at the thought of it. When this office disappeared, so did quality countercultural journalism—and a fair amount of superficial crap. So did my emergency shelter. With my rent due and bank account in the red, I envisaged dragging my mattress into the stairwell at Old Street and sleeping with the vendors. It really was imperative that I got out of London and earned some dosh.

On Friday, I had stolen a copy of *Vogue* from the Catford branch of WH Smith while high on mephedrone. When I saw a small item mentioning Gérard Derenne and his female entourage, I emailed Sizebank immediately. Like most correspondence sent under the influence of drugs and alcohol, I started to think this might have been a mistake.

"My train leaves in an hour," I said. "I need you to sign off my expenses for this story."

But the rumours about his cocaine-induced amnesia appeared to be true. "Which story?"

"The philosophy groupies."

"*Down N Out!* doesn't do philosophy."

"It's not about philosophy, it's not even about a philosopher," I assured him. "Check your emails."

"Gérard Derenne?" Sizebank got up and yawned. "Never heard of him."

Vogue described his entourage, colloquially known as the Derenne Femmes, as a cross between Charlie's Angels and Colonel Gadaffi's bodyguards. I had proposed *embedding* myself with them and writing a few thousand words. Given the success of my piece about the crack-smoking Tories, which had become a genuine news story (*Down N Out!*

didn't produce many), I didn't expect Sizebank to turn me down, or he would risk losing me.

"You know Hugh Woolley did a road trip around Europe for us?" he said. "It took him a month and he gave us ten-thousand words. His expenses were *fifty quid*. He got his mum to drive and take the pictures, and they slept in the back of the car. But you, you always ask for this, that and the other."

I didn't mention that unlike Hugh Woolley, I am working class and my mother doesn't subsidise my work expenses. I also write about much more significant topics than real ale. Nor did I mention the rumour that Woolley has a sexual relationship with his mother. In short, I remained professional.

"In 1999, or even 2009, I'd have booked you a hotel and given you a cocktail budget. But we can't do that anymore. I've got an embargo on all expenses except cover stories, and even then, we'd sweet talk a PR. This isn't a cover story. In fact, I'm still not convinced, what's the *Down N Out!* angle?"

An intern was trying to get Sizebank's attention from the other side of the turnstile. It was a co-ordinated distraction routine for when the subject of money came up. I followed them out into the office where the three remaining editorial staff were limbering up for the last editorial Ashtanga yoga session. Women's style editor Liz Fishlaw stood in front of the editorial whiteboard. "Palms together. Now fold, and drop the head."

Sizebank declared the warm-up over, dived onto the mat and pushed himself into a headstand. I stood nervously at the side, hoping my phone wouldn't die. I flashed the screen in front of his upside-down face. "I'm friends with her, she's working for him now," I said.

"Bring it closer, I can't see. And turn the screen around." I thrust the picture of the busty woman in his face. "Is that who I think it is?"

"Yes."

"Blimey, they're getting bigger every year. She was on the cover of our goth issue. I didn't know she was into philosophy."

"Me neither."

"Tim, keep your torso straight," Liz Fishlaw said.

The blood was sinking to Sizebank's head. My phone died in my hand. The Eurostar left in under an hour and I didn't have enough in my bank to buy another ticket. "Tim, is that a yes to the story?"

"Tim, keep your torso straight." Liz Fishlaw held onto his feet.

"Yes. I can pay you fifty quid for a blog and that's the lot."

"Tim, breathe in through the nose, out through the mouth."

I'd banked on 3,000 words at NUJ rate (33p a word) to clear my debts. Sizebank's proposed fee wouldn't even cover the cost of my train, and I would most likely lose my entitlement to Housing Benefit when I left the country. I thought back to what I'd heard while I was waiting. "What about if I brought you a cover story?"

"What does that look like?" Sizebank's face now purple, eyes rolling back.

"The philosopher, what if I brought you the philosopher?"

"*Down N Out!* doesn't do philosophy."

"He's been missing for months. Nobody's found him so far. Not *Le Monde*, the *Herald Tribune*, nobody." I didn't mention the fact that, for some strange reason, nobody else seemed to be looking. "It would put *Down N Out!* back on the map."

"We're already on the map, you cheeky fucker, 177 Old Street."

"Tim, your feet are cold, and oh my god, look at your face."

"Derenne's not just a philosopher." I put it in terms he would understand. "He's like Žižek crossed with Zidane out there."

"Sounds good," Sizebank said, short of air. "Anything else?"

"Just to confirm, it's 3,000 words at NUJ rate plus expenses?"

"Alright," Sizebank croaked. "Bring me the goods and the fee won't be an issue."

A sickening clicking sound came from his neck as Sizebank toppled backwards and his feet clattered into the editorial whiteboard, knocking it over. His chin was jammed against his shoulder, his body now a Ballardian mangle of broken plastic. He let out a monstrous roar of pain.

"Tamara, Hugo, help me lift him!" Liz yelped. "India, wet a snood for me!"

I thought about helping, but check-in for my Eurostar closed in fifteen minutes. As I was running out the door, the receptionist called out, "Hey, you. You're Lester Langway, aren't you? Why didn't you say? I love your work! Here are your magazines."

I stuffed them in my duffel bag.

"If you're going on assignment, I'll need to put a couple details in our system. What's your contact number?"

I palmed her the last of my business cards with a corner ripped off where I'd rolled a joint.

"Do you speak French?"

"Good enough to get by," I winked.

"And when will you be coming back?"

"A week," I said, and ran for the door.

V

Lester read along with Anaïs and smiled at his own ingenuity, the little exaggerations and flourishes that gave it more of a *literary* quality. "Waiter, two more beers."

Anaïs had big, shy eyes, the colour of autumn woodland, and they appeared to be saying, *you're either brave or stupid—probably both*. He did not, in fact, consider himself to be either, driven simply by an unexplainable compulsion.

For a student, her portfolio was impressive. Unlike the girls with arty parents who seem to have grown up with backstage passes sewn into their leather jackets, Anaïs's photo credits had yet to appear in print. So cripplingly self-conscious she often hid behind her forest of hair, he wondered if this withdrawn vantage was what made her photos of Parisian street life so special.

He lit a floppy cigarette, took a sip of his beer. "Are you up for doing the pictures?"

"I'm down with that," she shrugged.

"Do you have a long-lens or hidden camera?"

"Only this point-and-shoot." It was amazing to think that she could produce such quality with that old Olympus Trip 35mm made for tourists.

"No problem. I take most of my photos on disposables."

"When do you want me to do it? I have college three days a week and I'm working pretty much full-time."

"Where do you work?"

"The Rick Owens store."

"I thought he hired models to work in his stores."

"I'm only the toilet cleaner."

Lester brushed the stubble that was starting to appear on his neck in upwards motions, which made him feel aristocratic. "What if I paid you, say, fifty euros?"

"That would be great. When do you need me?"

"Between now and Sunday."

"Have you arranged the photo shoot?"

Lester downed his beer and ordered another. "I'm still waiting to confirm the details. I hope you'll be able to make it if we need to do it at the last minute." He checked his phone. He had a message from Tom Perkins. "Hold on a minute. I've got a lead. Alright, Anaïs, what are your plans for tonight?"

"Staring at the wall."

"Wrong. We're going to a party."

VI

He threw the last of his cash on the silver tray.

"Do you really think he'll be in?"

"That's not the point."

On the way, they checked at an Automated Terror Machine. "It's fine," he assured her, swiping his card from the slit. They looked in the shoe stores and even a branch of Monoprix, but there were none within his budget, and he refused to wear sandals. So they kept on with Lester hobbling down Boulevard Saint-Germain until they reached a row of Second Empire apartments. Anaïs didn't admire the palatial building as he did, but rather seemed disgusted by it.

"This is it. Now I wondered if you could do me a small favour?"

"You want me to take a picture of the front," she said, standing back from the coach gate.

"Not quite." He whispered into her ear what he wanted.

"Are you sure it will work?"

"You fooled me with the fire brigade. Just be confident."

She tossed her cigarette. "Sure. Which apartment?"

"My man could only find the street number."

"I guess we'll have to try them all until we get the right one."

"Actually, I read in a book about Baron Haussmann that before they installed lifts, apartments lower in the building were the most luxurious."

"That explains why I'm on the ninth floor."

"Start on the first floor."

Anaïs pressed herself up against the intercom as if about to kiss it, stuck her tongue out. He snapped a picture on his phone then pressed the buzzer.

"Hello?" the old housekeeper said.

"Oh, hello," Anaïs said. "This is Simone from ESCHATON Productions."

"Hello, Simone, is everything okay?"

"Yes, but I'm running around like crazy in this heat, and I don't have my diary with me. Can you remind me where the party is tonight?"

"Nobody tells me anything, dear. But if I had to guess, I'd say it's the same place as always, Café de Bore, is it not?"

Anaïs turned to Lester and gave him a mischievous grin. He wanted to hug her, but had read in a confidence manual about rationing praise to women, so he arched his brow into a serious v shape and nodded. "Pretty good." Grabbing him by the arm and tucking it into hers, Anaïs gave him one of her headphones and they skipped down the boulevard listening to 'Strip-Rock' by Magali Noël.

Fifty metres along, however, they felt a tap on their shoulders. It looked like the housekeeper. She was clutching a rolling pin dusted with flour, and looked extremely irate. "Madame, monsieur! Who are you?"

Heads waggling from side to side, they came to the same conclusion: run!

VII

The sun was dipping beneath the curving white maze of human traffic in the Latin Quarter. Tourists waddled by eating crêpes on the cobbles. Motorcycle couriers were loading pizzas into the back of heated boxes. Lester and Anaïs were still panting with adrenaline when they crashed into seats outside a bar on Rue de la Harpe.

Happy Hour had started at 5pm with two cocktails for ten euros. Lester would have a mojito and his photographer would take the same. "So how are you? How's college? And work? And your apartment?"

"I'm depressed."

"You're smiling."

"I've trained myself to smile when I'm sad."

"What do you have to be sad about?"

"I'm a mindless orphan with no purpose."

Lester got up and kicked an imaginary umbrella, music-hall style. "If you're depressed, move to London. Get a chihuahua on the NHS!"

"I don't want a dog, they're stupid. I'm getting a cat."

"Stupid things can still make you happy."

"Like what?"

"I'm looking at one."

"Pfft." Anaïs shook her head. She always had that look of fragile doom and disaster. There was something reassuring about it, like he knew she would be willing to drink with him into oblivion.

"Where are you staying, some fancy hotel?"

"Negative. A friend in Square du Temple."

"That's still fancy."

"Not exactly. I'm on the couch."

"You can crash at mine if you need to. I only have a single bed, but we're both skinny."

"I don't think that would be appropriate. Not if we're working," he said, and ordered two more mojitos.

"You can come over and take a bath."

He sniffed his armpits. "Are you trying to tell me something?"

"No, I take baths with all my friends. It's how we get to know each other."

Since moving to Paris from Brittany for her art and design course, she had clearly not made many friends.

VIII

One of Lester's few goals in life was to jump the queue and get into parties for free—that's why he had a press card. Although he didn't think it would hold much sway at the door of Café de Bore that night, where there was a scrum of young Gérard fans in Ralph Lauren chinos rolled up at the ankles, on the pavement at 10pm with their dates who'd been to finishing school. They were all hoping to get into the pre-Fashion Week party hosted by *Triomphe!*, the literary magazine Gérard had founded twenty-five years ago.

To get in before they did, Lester would have to give it that personal touch. Before he pushed to the front of the line, however, he noticed a young Marxist with pince-nez and a Soviet beret over an unwashed mop of hair, patrolling the line that stretched all the way around the block, handing out flyers from a paper-boy's satchel. "Fuck off with this trash!" A law student stamped a pamphlet into the gutter with her Dior shoes.

"Here, mate, I'll have one," Lester said.

He didn't have time to read it all, but was intrigued by the title: "GÉRARD: BOURGEOIS CAPITALIST TRAITOR. *Fraudulent 'philosopher' reigns over a territory much bigger than the Vatican—and is just as corrupt!*"

"Power to the working class!" Lester punched the air. "I'm a reporter from London covering the party. Not the *Party*, the party in there... Anyway, I want to include critical perspectives. Can I talk to you over here for a minute?"

"Which publication?" the young commie sneered.

"*Down N Out!*"

"Is that the rag sold by homeless comrades?"

"Yes, have you read it?"

"When I was in London for the Marxism Festival. It's filthy capitalist propaganda, exploiting the reserve army of labour. We invented guillotines for the likes of you!"

"Hold on a minute, pal. I'm part of the the reserve-army of labour myself. I don't even get a regular wage. From a strict class analysis, you could say I'm *lumpenproletariat*. So do me a favour. Tell me, why are you picketing the event?"

Having engaged with the Socialist Workers Party at their stall in Peckham once, Lester knew it didn't take much to convince a Trot to give you their two-pence worth.

"Alright, my name's Xavier. Let's start with the basic contradictions. *Triomphe!* claims to be a publication with a political conscience, confronting *barbarisms* such as torture and other human rights violations by foreign dictators. Look at that," he pointed to the poster of an Iranian prisoner draped from one of the baroque balconies. "Their activism, their virtuous campaigns, never touch upon their class privilege. Coincidence? As we all know, the system of wage labour is…"

"The ultimate mode of exploitation that enables all the others. Very interesting. Who's *they*?"

"Oh, it will be full of models, actors, magazine editors. Even our 'leftists' will be there, drinking champagne and eating snails, exposing their 'criticism' as a sham, a puppet show, phony dissent from within the accepted window of opinion."

"Sounds like quite a job I've got on my hands," Lester mused. He was unsure how he would recognise any of these people except the movie stars.

"I know, right? All these people for a magazine nobody reads! An elegant publication, most certainly, but in a quarter of a century, it has not brought a single idea to prominence nor discovered any authors of note."

"Why don't you venture inside, hand out a few pamphlets?"

"They would never let me in! I'm on their watch list, comrade."

"Whose watch list?" Lester quipped. "The Derenne Femmes?"

"Ever wondered why he is untouchable? No matter what the working class really thinks of him and his liberal filth, no matter how much the critics savage him, his image and his opinions are always front-and-centre in the press, radio, TV." A conspiratorial wink, or was it a twitch. "Those women, they're trained in the dark arts—

blackmail, honeytraps, kung fu."

"I'm sure they are." Lester had stopped taking notes and was desperate to go inside and use the bathroom. "Look, I've got to go in now, but why don't you give me a few of your leaflets and I'll scatter them around, see if I can turn a few over to our side."

"Absolutely, here you go." Lester stuffed a wad inside his Breton biography.

"It was lovely talking to you, brother. What's your number?" He gave Xavier his notepad and pen to write it down. "Hit me up, let's go for a drink some time." Despite his credentials, he could still be a humble working-class hero when he chose.

He grabbed Anaïs by the arm and dragged her to the front of the queue. An Editions Derenne tote bag clocked him on the shoulder. "Hey tramp, get to the back of the line."

Anaïs slapped the woman with her camera strap.

The entrance was guarded by two Algerian military men bulging out of tight-fitting black suits. Lester showed them his press card. A cursory look at the guest list showed that he most certainly did not belong there. "Go back to your shelter now," the muscle man said in a threatening voice.

It didn't matter if it was a fancy French café or Peckham jobcentre, Lester had never been able to keep his cool in the face of arbitrary rules. His face was reddened by drink and his pulse throbbed in his temples. Anaïs tugged at him to leave it, stop drawing attention to them. She shielded her face with her hair.

"This is my job, I'm supposed to be here." Lester peered beyond them to one of the most famous venues in Paris. He was curious about the place that was said to be not just a café, but an *intellectual climate*. Those who had made it past the gatepost were already displaying themselves arrogantly on the balconies, puffing cigarettes ostentatiously.

Another tote bag connected with him on the back of the head this time. "Monsieur, move back, we're more important than you."

Ordinarily, he might have tried another entrance, put on a hi-viz jacket or waiter's uniform, blagged his way in like that. But he'd been up since seven, drinking heavily on an empty stomach. Gins mixed with tequila-flavoured beer, then with a couple of litres of sugary mojito chucked in, his guts were now a sewer. It would have to be emptied sooner or later, so why not show these people the respect they deserved? He shuffled his right buttock to one side and let out most of the gas from his intestines, then tightened the screw. Like the chemical spray attack in *Goldfinger*, the weapon struck instantly. Fingers clinched around noses, shrill cries of "that's disgusting" pierced the rancid air as Lester stood silently, admiring his "SBD"— silent, but deadly.

The security parted, coughing and retching, as did the bourgeoisie. Rushing forward with Anaïs in tow, he didn't bother to check his bags or book in the cloak room, nor take the copy of *Triomphe!* one of the Femmes in a designer military-style dress was handing out at the door. They ran up the thickly carpeted stairs into a wonderfully decadent boudoir with streams of tropical plantation, gold-framed mirrors and cherubs on the walls. The distinguished crowd's suits and dresses were cut from cloths that muffled the acoustics of the jazz band. At the refulgent bar, bigwigs were sipping cognac from balloon snifters. "Is it an open tab?" Lester asked a lady clutching a chihuahua. She nodded. He pushed in alongside Charlotte Gainsbourg to order two gin and tonics.

"You didn't tell me we were coming to such a fancy place," Anaïs said.

"Don't worry, you look *chic*." She scowled at him. "Have you seen who it is?" He nodded to an amphibian in a white suit with streaked blonde hair.

"Oh my god, it's Johnny Hallyday."

"Sitting opposite?"

"Alain Delon?!"

"Come with me."

The gins were strong. When he pushed through the gangways between upholstered booths, clocking gallerists and models on the head with his bags, it seemed like everybody had been dissolved into two less potent versions of themselves. "Johnny!" Lester tugged on the pop icon's jacket. It seemed to have been greased with Vaseline, or perhaps he was melting in the heat that was hardly tamed by the fans blowing overhead. "Can I have a word?"

Johnny Hallyday's face was so stretched by Botox injections, he could neither smile nor frown. "Here's a word." The crooner scribbled an autograph on a napkin: "*Johnny.*"

Lester blew the hair off his forehead. "Mr Hallyday, in *Le Monde* last year, you predicted Gérard would achieve more fame with your musical collaboration, the *Monsieur Amour* LP, than as a philosopher. Will you be making any more music with him?"

Johnny hissed and carried on talking to Alain Delon, who had a pack of his own brand of cigarettes, discontinued in the 1980s, on the table. Lester pointed at them, made a casual smoking gesture. Delon tapped the pack and gave him one. He put it behind his ear and would either smoke it or sell it, depending how the next few days panned out.

Stalking the busy room, Lester gleaned that the man who wasn't there was the only topic of conversation that evening.

"Gérard's freedom comes first from his culture, and then because he's protected by his money."

"Anaïs, who is that?" Lester whispered.

"I don't know, I only read fashion magazines."

"And the books I recommend?"

She flashed him the copy of Céline he'd mailed her.

"Gérard would hate to be under the house arrest of a single identity," an elegant woman with white hair and tortoise-shell glasses said.

"He plays tricks with the truth."

"Have you been to the Châtelet yet and seen his history of the French Revolution?"

"Of course, we stayed for twenty-four hours. How did he produce such an epic alongside all his other commitments?"

"He only sleeps two hours a night. He even has more time than everybody else!"

"But there's also a professional schizophrenia, which means

he goes from an extremely pleasant life to dangerous situations in the field, and that's where he suddenly remembers the past. He has a great lucidity, and one of the explanations of his engagement is probably his refusal to be introspective, his quest for self being in going forward instead."

"He is moved by a feeling of fragility which pushes him to get closer to power, but he remains convinced that the story is tragic."

"In his younger days, Gérard was able to booze a little too much in the media and talk about both women's legs and the gulag. He played all the cards at once, which is not safe in a country like ours. He liked the media game, and never made an effort to extract himself from it, until now. While he was putting together his re-enactment of the French Revolution, I told him: 'Darling, you have to choose: do a philosophical play, or pose in magazines.'"

"It looks like he has finally made up his mind."

"Yes, but he is still a failed intellectual."

Lester stood fidgeting at the sidelines, waiting for a chance to interrupt. "Excuse me." The old snobs showed the shoeless little interloper their nostrils. "Did you really say that Gérard is a *failed* intellectual?"

"Absolutely not, monsieur!" Remembering these quotations from a *Monde Diplomatique* article, Lester snagged that he was talking to Gilles Hertzog, grandson of the Communist Party leader, a human rights activist and member of the *Triomphe!* editorial board. "I said he is a *field* intellectual. Anyway, who are you? What's your business here?"

"I'm a writer from London. I wondered," lowering his voice and stage whispering, as if on intimate terms, "why isn't Gérard coming tonight?"

They closed ranks, blocking Lester's access to their group. "Come on, Philippe, let's go and see if Depardieu or Belmondo have arrived yet." As they were shuffling away, Hertzog muttered something about the quality of the guest list being significantly worse than last time.

Then Lester saw a face he didn't expect to see here in a million years, a former colleague whose presence appeared to support those comments about the guest list. The kid was only nineteen and already notorious. He started as a computer hacker who leaked celebrity nudes, then landed himself a job as a technology news reporter. Lester's abiding memory of him from his brief stint at the *Daily Hack* was when he proposed running a "decapitation" story of a female reporter who had given a guy a handjob at their party, and he had surreptitiously filmed it. "But that's our job, Lester," he'd said in front of the rest of the staff. "We wreck lives."

He was the only person in the room dressed worse than Lester in his hoody and supermarket trainers, and obviously delighted to be on such a prestigious guest list. Lester buried his head in his armpit as his former colleague came towards him. "Oh my god, look who it is," the little shyster said to his partner, as if his former colleague couldn't hear him. "Lester Langway!" He'd brought along a wingman, a froggy little fellow with teenage acne who laughed at every insult and put-down. "Is this your girlfriend?"

"My photographer, Anaïs," Lester scratched his ear, grimaced, "meet Wilhelm Gnobb."

"Lovely to meet you, Anaïs, how do you know the legendary Lester Langway?"

"I met him at a party in Paris last year."

"Was he drunk?" Another thing Lester hated about Wilhelm was his outspoken teetotalism.

"He was pretty wasted, yeah," she laughed.

"So what are you doing here, Lester, besides drinking yourself into an early grave?"

"Working for *Down N Out!*"

"Oh yeah, how many magazines have you sold so far?" The wingman liked that one. A real thigh-slapper. Lester scraped his molars together, wanting to throw them both out of the window and onto the orchestra playing below.

"I'm working on a long-form essay about Gérard Derenne. You know who he is? He doesn't have a YouTube channel."

"Good one, Lester. I can see the booze hasn't slowed your quick wit. Always the funniest one in conference, weren't you? Do you think that's maybe why you were fired, because you were too witty? Is that what you tell your sources? I hear you don't have any sources. You don't even have any *friends*."

"Why do you call it a conference? It's a meeting. Whose approval are you seeking?"

"Ouch!" Wilhelm pretended to land a knockout blow on himself. "I'll give you one piece of advice for old time's sake. Whatever you do, don't waste your time chasing Gérard. I've already looked into this story, and I've got further than you would ever get. Trust me, there's nothing to see here. If you don't believe me, ask one of his staff, although I'm sure you've charmed them all already, haven't you? Good to see you, Lester. Keep reeling in those big fish. Oh, by the way," Wilhelm turned back to him. "Have you got a copy of the new *Triomphe!*? Here," he batted him on the chest with a rolled-up copy of the periodical. "I've got an opinion piece about internet freedom in it. If you can't read French, check out the translated version in the *New York Times*."

Lester ran out to the balcony and turned to the colophon on page two to check if Derenne's name was still there, but it wasn't. He took one look at Gnobb's essay, which had obviously been heavily edited, and ripped the page out. He set it alight and stamped on it, burning a hole through his socks. Then he tossed the remainder of his gin and tonic over his feet to kill the flames.

Anaïs threw herself at him and buried her head in his chest. "Are you okay? Here, I rolled you a cigarette."

"I'm in a nihilistic mood," he said, already smoking the Alain Delon fag.

"Is he a reporter like you?"

"We used to work together. He's the managing editor of Barkbite now."

"He's really young, isn't he?"

Lester resented that more than anything. It's wasn't so much the by-lines he was proud of, but how early he'd got them. "He hasn't even been to university, and you can tell. I had to show him the difference between a hyphen and a dash."

"How did he become an editor?"
"He has blackmail material on everybody."
"Even you?"
"Probably."

Back inside, Lester pointed to a darkened booth in the far corner where an oily, tanned fat man in a suit was being wafted by top-class escorts with peacock-feather fans.

"That's Steve Renault, the American media mogul and political consultant. He's Gnobb's boss. He's American, but he came to Britain and bought the *Daily Hack*. There's talk of him moving into Europe and starting reactionary papers here. If he does, you'll have a National Front government within the next ten years."

"Where is he? I can't see?" The lights had been dimmed to hide the identities of the shady characters.

"At the back, next to Roman Polanski." The diminutive Polish film director was propped up on cushions, stabbing at plates of crayfish with forks in his claw-like hands. Lester wanted to confront Polanski about what really happened at Cielo Drive on August 9th, 1969—the black Satanic hoods found at the scene, the dope deals... A couple more drinks and he might pluck up the courage.

"What's he doing here?"
"He fled America accused of sexual assault and rape."
"I meant Renault, not Polanski."
"I'm talking about Renault. There's a warrant out for his arrest in America, so he's over here—making friends with Gérard, of course." Before his disappearance, Derenne had spent a good many column inches pleading Renault's innocence and arguing that France should give him political refuge from the *barbarism* of the American penal system.

"Putain!" Anaïs said. "What did you bring me to, a party for rapists?"

IX

By 11pm, the jazz orchestra in the courtyard was in full swing, and Johnny Hallyday was crooning one of Lester's all-time favourites, 'Noir C'est Noir', or what could be made of it considering the singer's mouth barely opened. Leaning on the balustrade to keep himself from toppling over with a G&T in each hand, Lester belched. "While nobody's looking, snap a cheeky picture." She raised the Olympus point-and-shoot, brushed her hair to one side, squinted through the viewfinder. As her finger clicked and the camera made a mechanical whirring sound, a waiter tapped her on the shoulder. "Madame, no pictures of the famous people!"

"Alright," she shrugged, put the camera back in her satchel.

"Hey, look over there." Lester motioned with his head to the side of the bar. "Recognise her?"

"No, who is it?"

"Ridicula Goodman."

"The burlesque dancer. I've got her book at home."

"Yeah," he said as casually as he could. "She's my contact."

"You're serious?"

"More like a friend of a friend."

"Cool," Anaïs said, barely feigning enthusiasm. "Let me finish my cigarette."

Lester was disappointed by Anaïs's lack of interest in her subjects. He took it as an admission of defeat, when he didn't want a loser on his side. "Alright then, I'll have another, can you roll me one?"

The guy standing next to him looked like he belonged in a hair salon. In his skinny black suit, open-necked shirt and an absurdly pointed pair of winklepickers sans-socks, he was obviously homosexual. "Excuse me," Lester said with a roll-up dangling from his chops, "do you have fire?" He leaned into the flame and inhaled, held up the little torch. "So do you actually read *Triomphe!*?"

The man smacked his lips when he smoked. "I'm not really a big reader to be honest." Carlo Franzetti handed Lester his business card—Berluti: "Head of footwear."

"That's weird, I know a man who was foot of the headwear division."

The joke went over his head. "We basically designed all the clothes in Gérard's menswear collection."

"What did you design?"

"We did the white scarf, obviously, a black Gérard suit, and a silk bathrobe with the initials 'GD' on the nipple."

"I saw the ad for the underpants."

"Oh my god, yes, how could I forget?"

"Fair play, modelling them himself."

"I know, didn't he look stunning?"

"Wasn't he in his sixties?"

"I know, right? I hope I look that good when I'm his age."

Lester was getting bored of the superficial chitchat. He waited to be asked a question.

"So what brings you here?"

"I'm writing a piece for *Down N Out!* magazine."

"The homelessness magazine sold by fashion models?"

"The other way around."

"I'm sorry."

"People usually mistake me for one of the vendors."

"No offence, but you don't look like a model. You don't have the right bone structure."

"Nevermind," Lester sighed. "What was it like working for Gérard?"

"I never spoke to the guy, only his *entourage*."

"The 'Femmes'?"

"I dealt with a woman named Janice."

"What's Janice like?"

"Blonde, fortyish, some sort of academic. Our office used to call her the *colon*. Everything had to pass through her. All communications to and from him."

"Give me an example."

"When we were designing the smoking jacket, she'd send us a

note that said, 'Too much Hugh Hefner.' He'd list a bunch of random references. 'Less Sargent, more Renoir' or, 'this is Charles Dickens, I demand Rimbaud!' It drove us mad."

"Is she here tonight?"

"I haven't seen her. I'm not sure if she still works for him. I only came for free drinks."

"Do you have her contact?"

"Sure." Carlo tapped his phone against Lester's, and Janice's phone number appeared on his screen. "Watch out. Don't let him play games with you. Most people who deal with him end up with post-traumatic stress disorder."

"Awesome. I can't wait to meet her—or him."

"If you ever want to work again, I'd be careful if I were you." Carlo peeked inside to check who might be on the other side of the glass. "Gérard can ruin your life with a few words to the right people. Look around you, most of them are here. There are people who have learnt that the hard way, I'm *telling* you."

"You wouldn't happen to know where I might find them?"

"No. You would have to be very brave or very stupid to say anything publicly."

"About what?"

"Use your imagination. What does Gérard have that every woman wants?"

"Money?"

"Yes, and what else?"

"Power."

"Think he's on holiday, or in hiding?"

"I've already said more than I should. I signed an NDA. Please don't quote me in your article."

"Sorry I asked. It was good to talk to you."

Lester wanted to go to the bathroom and message Janice. "Wait," Carlo said. "Are you the guy that did the smelly fart downstairs?"

"Yeah, that's me."

"I got a whiff of it on the balcony. You should consider bottling it and selling it."

"I have your card."

"Respect," Carlo said. "You don't hear about smelly farts anymore. Keep up the good work."

Lester sprayed the air with Lynx Africa that he kept in a Chanel No. 5 bottle. Gave Carlo a fist bump. "SBV—silent, but violent. Anaïs, come over here and take a picture of me with this guy."

They posed and smiled. As they were heading back in, Lester said to Carlo out the side of his mouth: "I can't help but notice, I'm wearing socks without shoes, and you're wearing shoes without socks. Do you fancy swapping, just for a bit?"

"Sure, why the hell not!"

X

In a toilet cubicle, Lester examined the strangely shaped shoes he'd acquired. Not exactly winklepickers, they were like something a jester would wear, a cross between a slipper and a spoon. On the sole was the inscription, "Breton." Was it really that weird? There was, after all, a fashion brand called Céline, another of his favourite authors. Leafing through the biography to the photos, Lester couldn't see any pictures of the Surrealist's feet, but he found it hard to believe that a *flâneur* would walk the streets of Paris in such an uncomfortable shoe. They slid off his heels when he picked them up and pinched his toes when he put them down. Jamming his fingers inside to see what was digging into the inside arch, he found a miniature envelope. He rubbed some of the white powder into his gums, and when he felt them numbing, he knew this was just what he needed. When he waddled out of the men's room, he was already starting to gurn.

As Giorgio de Chirico once described Paul Eluard, Lester presented himself with a face somewhere between that of an onanist and a mystical cretin. From her bar stool, Ridicula Goodman towered over him with her flames of orange hair, business jacket over a black whale-bone corset, huge hooters that seemed to absorb the soft light, and a look of bafflement. Did she recall where this importunate young man might have come from? "Of course I remember," she said finally, clinging onto a male companion who smiled with the determination of a man at a party drinking water. "Etienne, this is Luke? Leroy?... a friend of a friend from London."

"Lester Langway," he reminded her, and signalled to the barman for another gin. "We met last year—at Frederic's pad."

"Are you sure it was Frederic's pad?"

"On the steps outside Stolly's. Then we all went back to Freddy's place in Square du Temple. We were pretty wasted."

Quickly changing the subject... "Etienne won the Café de Bore Prize for literature. He's on the new editorial board for *Triomphe!* Did you get one at the door?"

"I did, but I seem to have misplaced it."

"Here, have another."

Lester rolled it up and put it in his back pocket, the way a builder would with a copy of the *Daily Sport*. "Thanks. I'll read it when I get home."

"You absolutely should read Ridicula's piece about transgender women," Etienne said in a deep, conceited voice. "It's so honest, so insightful of what it means to be beautiful."

"Actually, I read Ridicula's book when it came out in the spring." He'd browsed through a review copy of *Afternoon Tease* in the *Down N Out!* office and thought it was garbage. "On the whole I enjoyed it."

"Thank you, what did you like about it?"

"The pictures were my favourite part."

"That's... good to know."

"You should get a proofreader. I spotted a couple of spelling errors." Etienne stepped forward to defend his woman's pride, but Ridicula's biceps were bigger. She shrugged him aside. "I'm sorry, I didn't mean it like that!"

"And what do *you* do, exactly?"

"I'm working for *Down N Out!*"

"Really, well, I guess we all have to start somewhere."

"Writing for it, not selling it."

"Oh."

"What I meant to say is, your work deserves respect. God knows I've had my problems with mistakes being edited into my copy. Would you like some cocaine?"

"You have some?" On hearing the magic word, Ridicula's face changed from thunder to sunshine. She checked with Etienne. "Baby, do you mind?" Then back to Lester. "Sure." Leading him eagerly down the stairs... "I'm not offended, don't be silly, *of course* you were right to point it out to me, from one professional writer to another..." Her touch giving him shudders of excitement, the Canadian burlesque star confided, "Etienne had a problem. He's been to recovery. But he doesn't mind if I dabble every now and then."

Dragging him into the women's bathroom, Ridicula slammed the door and jammed the lock. There was something vampiric about her, a force that was overwhelmingly powerful and alluring. When Lester produced the little envelope and started to unwrap it, Ridicula bit down on her blood-red lip. To share this intimate, illicit experience with such a titan of desire, and to be in possession of something she wanted, made him the envy of millions of men. His hands shook as he scraped the crumbles out of the wrap with his Lobster card. Ridicula crowded over him and he smelt the obscure scents on her neck. Her breasts cushioned up against him. "Are those lines big enough?"

"Pretty big. You want more?"

"I always start with a huge one to set me going."

He scraped another portion towards the two snowy mounds. She was transfixed by the drug. "A little more." There was no use objecting, he knew he would do anything for her. "That should do." She already had a banknote rolled up, poised, ready to go. As soon as it was prepared into two neat lines, she eased Lester out of the way. After taking aim, she hoovered hers up in a single, lightning-fast movement of the head, a barely audible sniff. Any quicker and she would have noticed him taking a snap on his phone. He slid it back into his pocket coolly, expertly, and breathed a sigh of relief.

Calmer now, he took a little more time over his line, deciding which side to attack it from. Ridicula pinched her nose and shuddered. "So is Tim Sizebank still behind the wheel?"

Bent over the toilet bowl, he said: "He is, unfortunately."

"I *love* Tim, he's one of my favourite people in fashion."

"He's been good to me. And he loves the naughty chalk."

"Oh, I know, tell me about it. Once he starts, he can't stop."

Through the open window, they could hear Charles Aznavour singing over a marimba. "There are hardly any staffers left, and I'm the only reporter with an expense account because I'm writing the cover story. It's actually about Gérard, so I wondered if you might know..."

"I heard it's going down the pan. Or what is it you Brits say, *tits up*?"

Lester bounced his eyes up to her chest, looming over him like planets, and back again. Then, finally, he dived in and took his hit.

"If it does, I can just as easily pitch it to *Esquire* or *GQ*," he said, neglecting to mention that they had never responded to any of his previous emails.

The drug had hit Ridicula's brain. She was starting to jitter. "That's some good shit, where'd you get it from?"

"I found it in my... achoo!" Lester pinched his nose to keep from spilling any, eyes reddening a little. "I found it in my shoe."

"Aww, that's cute." She ruffled his hair. "A proper street kid, aren't you?"

He'd read in her book how she liked to play with skinny rockers and starving artists. He snarled at her, pushed her back against the toilet wall—like a young Jean-Paul Belmondo would have done. He grabbed for her breast and got a big, soft handful—*holy electric jellyfish!*—and lunged upwards to take a bite out of her mouth. When she pulled away, he figured she must have been play-acting like in the horror movies she ripped off for her aesthetic. He pulled her toward him and tried again. But she removed his hand delicately and pushed him away. "Sorry," she said. "I didn't ask for that."

"I'm sorry," he said.

"It's okay, don't worry about it," she said as they were leaving.

Climbing up the stairs, he tried to convey an air of normality as he dabbed at his nose. "What is it you do for Gérard? I'm trying to piece together some background before our interview. It would be great to chat to you some time, seeing as you're obviously so articulate and insightful."

"I'm a producer," she said over her shoulder.

"Fancy a drink some time this week?"

"Maybe," she said and rushed off through the crowd to chat her head off to her bloke.

XI

On the way back from the bogs, he found Anaïs sitting on the floor, uninterested in her surroundings, reading the *Diagnostic and Statistical Manual of Mental Disorders* (DSM-5). "Look who it is!" He tried to enthuse her, but to no avail.

An audience had gathered around a slim, spiky-haired man in a tight-fitting tshirt. "It's Uri Geller!" Much to the concern of the head waiter, who was hovering nearby anxiously, as the famous mentalist had located the cutlery.

The audience must have seen this trick before, as he was world famous for it, but that only added to their delight. "Ladies and gentlemen, keep your eyes on the spoon." Uri Geller stared at the coffee spoon with great intensity.

Scanning the room, Lester noticed Gérard Depardieu propped up in a regal chair with a huge goblet of red wine, hypnotised by Geller's performance. Charlotte Gainsbourg and Vincent Cassel were wide-eyed, transfixed. "Now I am going to rub the spoon, ever so gently, like this." Moments passed. The ultimate showman, Geller knew how to manipulate the psychic ether. Then, sharp intakes of breath as the finest steel cutlery succumbed to the slightest of touches. It was an astonishing demonstration of Uri Geller's psychic powers. Gasps, cries, followed by an increasing intensity of applause as the spoon continued to bend, apparently of its own free will, in the hot summer air.

There was only one eyeball not transfixed by Uri Geller and his spoon. Beneath a head of tightly parted dark hair, the same uni-glare he'd felt earlier, at the Bureau, was fixed upon him like a laser beam. When Lester caught her eye, another one of the Derenne Femmes appeared at her side, this one dressed in civilian clothes. They were dotted all around the room now, these women with earpieces. He gathered that they weren't here to have fun—they were on duty. Had they been watching him all night? Listening in on the microphones Gérard liked to put in bathrooms?

Lester pushed through the crowd, heartbeat pounding, and accosted the magician. "Can I speak with you for a minute, Uri? It's urgent."

As a psychic, Geller obviously shouldn't have needed to ask what it was about, but he did anyway. "This is a private gathering, I'm among friends, I feel slightly uncomfortable about you coming up to me like this," Geller said in his strange, high-pitched voice. "What's so urgent, may I ask?"

Lester apologised to Charlotte Rampling, whose fawning praise he had interrupted. "Uri, give me two minutes and I'll leave you alone, I promise. There's something really eerie going on around here."

"Excuse me a moment, ladies and gentlemen, this young man needs my help. I'll be right back."

Uri led him into a private side-room. One of Gérard's movies was screening on the wall. The place was empty.

"I must warn you, this is very risky behaviour you're engaging in, son," Uri Geller said, locking the door behind them.

"What behaviour? Is it obvious? Can you tell me what I've done?"

Uri tapped his fingers on Lester's temples and told him to close his eyes. "I have given psychic advice to some of the world's greatest artists. Elvis, Michael Jackson, Gérard. They were all motivated by one thing, besides their genius. Dissatisfaction with how things were. They wanted to improve themselves, be the *best* they could be. This is also true of you, is it not?"

Lester felt an extraterrestrial calm about the place now. Uri had transported him to a higher plane of existence. "You're absolutely right."

"Because you are an artist, you have come to Paris, like so many great artists before you. I cannot tell, since I have only spent a few moments with you, whether you are going to become a great artist, although let me reassure you that anything is possible if you *truly believe* it. If you *truly believe* something, you have the power to change reality."

Lester's breathing slowed down.

"You have come to Paris to find somebody special, am I right?"

"Absolutely bang on." Lester opened his eyes. "Can you tell me where he is, Uri?"

Uri looked him square in the eyes. "Son, I do not know your name, I think I know who you are talking about."

"G—"

"No, I don't want to hear it." Uri shushed Lester's lips with his finger. "It's not important. You will not find him until you find yourself, my son. Do you hear me? Find yourself. Do *whatever* you have to do in order to achieve it. That is my advice to you. Now be on your way."

XII

When he left the cinema room, they were waiting for him. He tasted the cocaine in the back of his throat. "Owen Appletree, is it?"

The woman had a phone in a leather flip case that wouldn't stop vibrating. She reminded him of Laura Kuenssberg, the BBC political reporter who seemed to exemplify everything he was not: moderate, controlled, serious, sober. The Femme with the eyepatch lingered in the background, and another young Femme with an earpiece watched from behind the glass door of the restaurant.

"Yes, and you are?"

"Simone Gordon, executive producer, ESCHATON Productions. Lydia tells me you came by the Bureau earlier today."

"That's right," he smirked.

"I'll ask again, what's your business?"

"Like I told your colleagues earlier, I'm writing a piece about the Surrealists. What's your business, are you involved with this literary magazine?"

"We don't have anything to do with *Triomphe!* anymore."

"Really?" He scoffed at the absurdity of such a statement, with his entourage swarming. "Gérard edited it for twenty-five years."

"This may or may not be the last issue."

"Why's his name not on the colophon?"

"If Gérard is involved, it will be in an unofficial capacity. But like I said, we can neither confirm nor deny his involvement. If you have any questions, please email them to info@eschatonproductions.com and it is unlikely anybody will get back to you."

Ms Gordon watched impatiently while Lester noted it down, eager to get to the real issue. "Point number two. Maybe you should write this down and underline it. Gérard's private residence is *strictly off limits*."

"Private residence? Where would that be?"

"You and your partner dropped by earlier today and bothered his housekeeper, Madame Delaroux, who is eighty-nine years old.

She informed us that your partner is also named Simone Gordon, am I correct?"

"I am not at liberty to give out third-party information," Lester sniggered. "Third-party *imitation*, however..."

"For the avoidance of doubt, Mr Appletree, we would like to remind you that if you bother any of Gérard's family, friends or properties again, there will be dire consequences for you."

"Hold on, let me write that down. *Dire... con-se-quen-ces*."

"I would also like to remind you that subterfuge contravenes the journalistic code of ethics."

He made it an elaborate performance, taking note of these threats. "*Jour-na-lis-tic code of eth-ics*. I didn't realise I was talking to the *Columbia Journalism Review*."

"Actually, I was an editorial intern on the *CJR*. I still write for them from time to time. *And* I learned shorthand."

"Well in that case, aren't *you* performing a kind of subterfuge?"

"Mr Appletree, I am not currently reviewing your reporting, and I hope you give me no reasons to do so."

"I am not currently reviewing your threats or intimidation tactics. I'm sure we'd both like to keep it that way, wouldn't we?"

"Absolutely, Mr Appletree."

"Well in that case, why don't I cut you a deal?" The cocaine must have changed his state of mind somewhat, made him more confrontational.

"I'm not sure I understand what you are offering, or perhaps threatening."

"Oh it's quite simple," Lester tried to retain a wistful air, but conveyed aggression and menace. "I won't mention your threats if you answer a couple of questions."

"Lydia, can we escort Mr Appletree to the bar?"

"Alpha, Delta, Romeo to the cinema," Lydia said into her cufflink.

Three other Femmes appeared in designer military-style clothes with earpieces. They didn't quite exude Lydia's menace, but they formed a tight cordon around Lester and marched him to the waiter's station. Thankfully nobody noticed this embarrassing scene, as Uri Geller had everybody hypnotised.

"Marcel, show Mr Appletree the damage." A moustachioed man in an apron, struggling to unbend a spoon, pushed a silver tray with a long, curly receipt on it across the counter. "How would you like to pay, monsieur? Cash or card?"

A hundred and forty euros! Had they really downed that many drinks? Surely not. At least he'd got a nose full of cocaine into the bargain. Still, on a point of principle he refused to pay. He screwed the receipt up and threw it on the floor.

"Mr Appletree, we strongly advise you not to leave the café without paying. It is a criminal offence."

"Fuck off, it's a free bar."

"A free bar for *invited guests*, Mr Appletree."

He didn't believe Gérard or Steve Renault or whoever was backing the shindig would care about the money. But by using his card, he would reveal his identity. This was a very sneaky tactic. And there seemed to be no getting out of it without assaulting a woman.

"Mr Appletree, is everything okay?"

He stood for a moment massaging his temples as Uri had done. "Yes," he said, "I'm just trying to remember my pin number." He heard Uri's voice in his head, telling him to do whatever he had to do in order to succeed. In the background, Uri was bamboozling the guests with a wristwatch.

"Look at the watch, ladies and gentlemen. The time is currently three minutes past midnight. Three minutes one second. Three minutes two seconds. Three minutes three seconds. Now ladies and gentlemen, I am going to ask you to close your eyes and follow my instructions. Breathe in, breathe out. Breathe in, breathe out. Now if you open your eyes, you will see that the time is still three minutes and three seconds past midnight. Slowly, slowly, three minutes, three seconds and a quarter. Three minutes, three seconds and a half..."

Uri made evocative hand gestures at the watch, waggling his fingers, flicking cosmic energy at it.

As soon as they set eyes on the slowed-down watch, the Femmes and the maitre'd's mouths hung open and they became transfixed, suspended in time. Lester used this opportunity to sneak away.

Anaïs was still reading her book with headphones in, unphased by Uri's hypnotic spell. He caught her mid-yawn. "Come on, let's bust a move."

"Is everything okay?"

"It's fine. But whatever you do, don't pay any attention to Uri Geller."

"Alright, I wasn't planning to."

All the people in the café besides Lester and Anaïs were frozen, statuesque, so they were able to walk in between these figurines, completely unnoticed and unphased by the psychic spell that had set them in place like upright cadavers.

Lester grabbed their half-finished glasses from the tables, necked them, and tossed revolutionary leaflets into the air on his way out. "Get a load of that, you filthy lizards!" he screamed, and the sound of gunshots rang out in the streets. They ran downstairs, through the bar and out the door with revolutionary Marxism floating through the air like confetti.

Their veins were full of champagne when they spilled onto the Boulevard Saint-Germain. With a full moon overhead, Lester vomited onto the flowers in the Jardin du Luxembourg.

He clutched onto Anaïs as they headed for the Métro. "It's like Inspector Maigret said. Is it my fault..." hiccup "...if you sometimes have to drink with people to see what makes them tick?"

"No, darling, but you don't have to get quite so shitfaced?"

"Bah."

On the Métro, he looked at their reflections in the glass. She'd slumped her head on his shoulder. "Do you want to stay at my place? We can take a bath together."

Ahh! She was already talking to him like a wife.

TUESDAY

XIII

By the time most people were due in the office, the flashing green signs outside pharmacies showed the temperature in Paris was already thirty degrees. From the balcony of the 9th floor apartment, Lester could see all the way to the Sacré-Cœur in the northern quarter of Montmartre. The city was dazzling, a disordered sprawl of white glare.

Below them in the square, Chinese men were performing tai chi on the bandstand and the ping pong tables were already occupied. Freddy staggered back into the kitchen to fetch more wine and rewind the song of the evening, 'Intoxicated Man' by Serge Gainsbourg. Now Lester regretted bailing on Anaïs at Republique with an air kiss. His intention was not to be rude, but appear enigmatic. Now, however, he was paying the price for it.

He had bundled through Freddy's door on Rue de Bretagne at 00.47am to find the ginger-haired comedian sitting in boxer shorts and Wu-Tang Clan tshirt, drinking white wine alone in his two-room rooftop studio. Once they'd finished the gram Lester brought with him, they couldn't control their urge for more, and so Lester emptied his bank account to go halves on another two. They whiled away the hours until dawn prank-calling pizza companies, cab offices and prostitutes. Then Freddy concocted a devious scheme that put his talents to use for Lester's story. He did two snow-plough lines off the breakfast tray he'd nailed to the balustrade before starting work.

"Are you sure this is such a good idea? I mean, it was a bit of an awkward situation last night." Lester sniffled, feeling a nosebleed coming on.

"You didn't fuck her, did you?"

"No."

"Did you try?"

"No."

"What is there to worry about, then?"

He wiped the suncream onto his shorts and grabbed for the

phone, but Freddy insisted that he had to speak to Ridicula again. The last time he'd seen her was last year, at this pad.

"Allo! Allo!" Freddy said in a panicked tone, palming Lester away. "Ridicula? It's Gérard. Sorry to have woken you. I'm in an emergency situation. I need your help, right away. It can't wait."

Lester had to admit, it wasn't a terrible impression. If you didn't know Freddy, he could have passed for a hysterical French intellectual making an SOS call to a dominatrix.

"I went for a walk in the countryside. I got caught in a storm."

"..."

"It may not have rained in Paris but it was very stormy here."

"..."

"Yes, it's a microclimate."

"..."

"Please stop interrupting! I came into a barn to shelter and got locked in. Are you still there? Good. I don't know how to say this. I'm in so much agony. There is a machine here for milking the cows. I was bored and lonely, so I put my penis in it. I just thought it would feel good. I switched it on and now I can't switch it off. Ah! No! It's starting again! Ridicula, no, please don't go, this is a matter of life and death! Try to get the farmer's... Ridicula, are you there...?"

Lester was unsure of whether to laugh or cry. Freddy refilled his wine and held up a toast, as though the entire city was applauding him, took a bow. "The net is closing around him, my friend!"

"Is it?" Lester couldn't stand to look at his gloating friend, who did not respect the seriousness of the situation. "Do you really think so? Can you explain how that... what was it, a joke you just made up?"

"No, I didn't make it up."

"What is it, then?"

"Jim Davidson."

"What has happened?" Lester wondered, trying to keep his brains from falling out. "I'm supposed to be an investigative journalist. Why am I authorising my drunk mates to call female sources and tell them Jim Davidson jokes? I don't understand how it came to this."

"Lester, you're not thinking like Maigret."
"Evidently not. What would Maigret think?"
"What can we learn from the call?"
"Old-fashioned British comedians are making a comeback?"
"You're supposed to be the detective."
"I've been up too long. I can't think anymore."
"What did Ridicula appear to know?"
"The weather in Paris?"
"Exactly."
"And what didn't she believe about my story?"
"That Gérard is dumb enough to put his dick in a milking machine?"
"Besides that."
"It rained last night."
"Go on."
"Because it didn't rain here."
"Yes..."
"So you think Gérard is in the countryside not far from Paris."
"Voila!"

It was as good a theory as any, and it saved him from going to Marrakesh, or Algiers to look for the philosopher—although he wouldn't have minded a trip down to the Riviera this time of year. Tom Perkins should be able to locate his country addresses and those of his close associates. But in terms of compelling Gérard to speak, Lester still had plenty of reporting to do.

He slumped in his chair, wiped his brow, breathed out. Now he wondered if he had transgressed too much, too soon. He still needed to reassure himself that he was not a total fool. So he did another line of coke, poured himself another glass of wine, fetched Freddy's laptop and started writing.

XIV

In certain ways, Lester's correspondence with Sizebank reflected the same restless search for a mentor that had been evident in his schoolboy letters to Rimbaud and Apollinaire. He wrote to tell him of his tastes in literature, art and film, and rejoiced at being able to "reveal" to his editor "something of the work of my friend Paul Valéry." Feeling extremely lucid and emotionally open, he continued to shower his editor with verbiage. "I'm experiencing an instant of delightful turmoil. You are precisely the friend I was expecting at this time in my life."

A few seconds later, Lester's inbox pinged. "The work of Paul Valéry? Fuck off."

He did another line of coke off a Brian Jonestown Massacre album cover to give him the courage to call his bad-tempered editor.

"Sizebank."

"Tim, it's Lester. How's your neck?"

"Agony. What do you want?"

"Just calling to update you on the piece. I have cultivated a couple of strong sources, and my attempts at geolocation are progressing very nicely."

"What piece?"

"The one we discussed yesterday."

"Oh. Hold on, let me have a butcher's." There was a creaking sound on the other end of the line, flesh against pleather. "Liz," he yelled, "do you remember commissioning anything by Lester Langway? Come here. You speak to him."

"Tim..."

"Hello, Lester, this is Liz. Tim has concussion, short-term amnesia and minor spinal damage after his yoga accident yesterday. His neck's in a brace, he's on strong pain medication and he has limited mobility. I've just checked the editorial spreadsheet, and we don't have anything down by you I'm afraid."

"You what? Tim gave me the sign off for this piece—a cover

story about Gérard Derenne. You were there, you must have heard."

"I saw you in the office, Lester. You stood by and watched while Tim nearly died in that headstand. I don't recall any agreement about a story, I'm sorry." The lying bitch. Then from the distance, Sizebank yelled: "Liz, Tell him I've reread the original pitch he sent us, and it's a pile of shit. We'll give him a ten-percent kill fee."

"Did you hear that?" Liz said.

"Um, this makes no sense. Ask Tamara on reception. I gave her my phone number because I was going away *on commission*."

"Lester, we never confirmed this piece."

"But Tamara..."

"Feel free to place it elsewhere."

"How can you offer a *kill fee* if you never offered me a fee in the first place?"

"What was the fee, Lester?"

"Nine hundred and ninety-nine quid plus expenses. If you could pass me back to Tim, I'm sure he'll be happy to send me a small advance."

"Tim says the only fee he mentioned with you was fifty."

"That was for a different, shorter piece for the web. This is a major investigation for print. You were there yesterday when he said, 'Bring us the goods and the fee won't be an issue.' And I'm calling to tell you, I'm bringing you the goods, but I can't do that when I don't have a cent in my bank account.'"

"Send us an invoice for five. We'll pay as soon as we can, usually within ninety days. Is there anything else?"

"I hope your periods are painful."

He squeezed the phone as hard as he could, growling and yelling to himself, clocking himself over the head with his fists.

XV

If necessity is the mother of invention, then desperation must be its father. Lester took a swig of wine and ground his molars together. He'd put on a colonial-style helmet to protect himself from the sun—and his own fists. He was shaking with rage when he found the little knobsplash's number.

"Hello Wilhelm." Trying to play it cool like Roger Moore… "it's Lester Langway."

"Lester, my man, how's the hangover?"

"*Terrific*. Just admiring the Sacré-Cœur while I have breakfast *al fresco*."

"I'm in the middle of wrecking somebody's life. I don't have time for alcoholic confessions. Why don't you check out an AA meeting?"

"Fuck you. I've got a big splash."

Wilhelm sighed. Lester gripped the phone hard, cupping his hand over his mouth in fear, trying not to breathe too heavily. "Go on then, what have you got?"

He really didn't want to do this, but given the desperate situation *Down N Out!* had put him in, he really had no choice but to cash in the only asset he had now that he'd smoked that Alain Delon cigarette. "I've got an exclusive picture of Ridicula Goodman doing illegal drugs."

There was a short silence on the end of the line. He knew Wilhelm wasn't averse to this kind of dirt—in fact, hidden-camera stories were his specialism. The issue was whether he would want to deal with Lester again.

"Fair enough, send it across via encrypted message."

"Done."

"Okay, Lester, it's good. How much were you thinking?"

"A thousand euros," Lester said.

"Five hundred."

"It's a deal—on one condition. You don't publish for at least a week."

"Don't worry Lester, I'm not going to publish it this week."

"Great," Lester thought, he's probably going to keep it in his desk drawer, like he does with his other kompromat. "When can you pay?"

"I'm sending it over now in Bitcoin, if that's okay?"

"I have no objections to that."

"You should receive a confirmation in twenty minutes."

"Thanks. Good to work with you again, Wilhelm."

He stood up and punched the sky. What a deal, he thought to himself. He had turned defeat into victory, saving himself with his own ingenuity. Even the seediness of it felt good, like he was a proper Fleet Street gumshoe.

XVI

Now he was on a roll, why stop there? When Freddy came back from the pool, he kissed his arse and gave him the phone.

"Hello, Tim Sizebank."

"Bonjour," Freddy said, still dripping with pool water. "I am looking for the editor of *Down N Out!*"

"Who's looking?"

"This is Gérard Derenne, the philosopher."

"We don't do philosophy."

"I am looking for your reporter, Mr Langway. I would like to grant him an interview for your publication."

"Alright, Gerald. Leave us your number and we'll get back to you."

Sizebank yelled and passed the phone over to Liz.

"Monsieur Derenne, it is an honour to speak with you." Lester stuck his fingers down his throat and retched at her phoney French accent. "We would be honoured to arrange an interview with one of our *senior editors*. Seeing as I am familiar with your stunning work with Berluti, I would be happy to conduct the interview myself—at a location of your choice, of course—and arrange a photo shoot."

"Thank you, madame, but it is your writer I was hoping to speak with."

"That is much appreciated, monsieur. But I was actually at your runway show in Paris. I even mentioned it on one of my social media accounts. Our November cover is currently free, so I would love to set this up, if you have any dates available in the coming weeks?"

"I am sorry madame, I am sure you are a wonderful journalist, but I was specifically looking to speak with Mr Langway. He met my dear friend Jacques Dutronc yesterday and made an excellent impression. No offence to you, but he is a really terrific writer, you are most fortunate to have him in your pages. It would be an honour for me to work with such a special talent, a star for the future."

Liz sounded suitably embittered. "I will see if we have his number and pass a message on."

"Would you please do that as a matter of urgency? I hear he is only in Paris for one week, and I am also very busy. I would hate to miss him."

"We will endeavour to do that, Monsieur Derenne."

"I am sorry, endeavour is not quite good enough. Can you *promise* me you will message him and say that I am looking to speak with him for a *Down N Out!* cover feature?"

"Yes, Monsieur Derenne, I promise we will be in contact with him, and will pass on your message. Although I have to insist that our photo shoot will be handled by a member of the..."

"Thank you. That is all I ask. Goodbye."

XVII

With his mind finally at ease, Lester was able to sit back and look at the bigger picture. The Breton biography was open on his lap, and he squinted at the pages streaked by shadows of the balustrade, lost in a dizzying spiral of possibilities. What universal force had propelled him from Dutronc's office to the Bureau of Surrealist Research, connecting him to ESCHATON Productions and the *Triomphe!* party? Had the book been placed there deliberately, at the top of the stack by his feet—and if so, why?

Freddy tossed a Marlborough into his mouth and started to eat it. "What would Maigret do?"

"Maigret wouldn't still be up at ten in the morning doing gak."

"True."

"But maybe that's why I'm the superior detective."

Now they were open, Lester dialled the Philosophy department at the Sorbonne. In his coked-up mind, the phone seemed to ring for an unbearable amount of time before a secretary answered. "Hello madame, I'd like to speak to Professor Jacques Dutronc."

"Who's calling?"

"Lester Langway, *Down N Out!* magazine. Urgently."

"I'm sorry, monsieur, Jacques Dutronc doesn't work here."

"What? You must be joking. Hold the line..." Lester covered the earpiece with his hand. "She's saying they've never heard of him. Can you do me a favour and load their website?" Back on the phone: "One moment, madame, we're just checking something."

Freddy held up the staff page of the website on his laptop. Lester scrolled up and down. There was no Jacques Dutronc listed in the Philosophy department.

Lester asked them to check the directory, read out the titles of his books, described his physical appearance, the location and décor of his office. The woman insisted that he was not a member of staff at the Sorbonne. "Good day, monsieur."

"Good fucking day?!" Lester screamed.

A man in the square holding a dirty sock yelled back, "Good fucking day?! Are you the one throwing socks off the balcony?"
"Fuck you!"
"Fuck me?! You hit me in the face!"
"Wasn't me!"

XVIII

The cocaine in Paris was some of the strongest he'd ever had. It was almost midday, and Lester still had an uncontrollable urge to jabber. Preferably somebody he didn't despise, and who didn't despise him. He called Anaïs.

"Hey, do you want to come over to Square du Temple?"
"Have you been to bed yet?"
"No."
"Are you going to?"
"I don't think so."
"I just woke up with the worst hangover."
"What are you doing later today?"
"I'm supposed to go on a date with Julien Badbeger."
"Who?"
"The novelist I met at the party last night. He's very handsome. And he has a beard."
"How did this happen?"
"He asked for my number while you took your *friend* to the toilet."

Lester did a quick internet search. She was right, he was handsome, he'd won a lot of prizes—and he had a beard. "You want to watch out for him, he's got a bit of a reputation."

"You're not jealous, are you?"
"I have a moral responsibility to protect my photographer, that's all. Make sure your phone's charged, and don't let him take you anywhere without a signal. If you suspect anything dodgy, call me straight away."

"Don't worry, Lester, I've been on dates before."
"Good. While you're there, can you do some digging for me?"
Anaïs sighed. "Do you want me to take a notepad?"
"No, but you might want to take a Dictaphone if you have one."
"I'm not going to record my date, you idiot."
"Fair enough. But any information about Gérard, previous

conduct, why he fled, and where to… I'm looking into this Badbeger character now, and they appear very close. He's bound to know something, and he won't be as cautious with you as he would be with me."

"True."

"Does he know you work for me?"

"I didn't even know I worked for you."

"You know what I mean. Does he know we're friends, that you're taking pictures for my article?"

"I didn't mention it, no."

"But that doesn't rule it out. He might be looking for dirt on me. Beware of that."

"Lester, you're overthinking things. It's just a date."

"Maybe."

"Have you been taking drugs?"

"A little."

"I can tell."

"One more thing. What are you going to wear?"

"I hadn't thought about it, why?"

"He seems to like women who are taller than him. Are you going to wear heels?"

"I only have two pairs of shoes, Converse and Dr Martens."

"I prefer the black DM's on you."

"I can't believe you're telling me what to wear on a date."

"Admit it, you like it."

"I do."

"Good."

"Anyway, what are you doing later?"

"In case your date doesn't go to plan, you mean? Plan B?"

"Yeah."

"I'm meeting a source."

"Oh yeah?" She sounded more amused than jealous, which annoyed him. "Who with?"

"I can't say, it's supposed to be top secret."

"I'm not going to tell anybody. Is it the one with the big tits again?"

"No, the one with big brains."

XIX

At three in the afternoon, Lester had a pain between his temples from reading the Breton biography in the sun for too long. He popped two prescription cocodamols with one of his antidepressants, swilled them down with the last dregs of wine, and stayed face down on Freddy's bed for half an hour. Finally up, he made himself an espresso, squeezed out a shit that came out hard and crisp like a diamond and smelled like something the military would use. He jumped in the shower, cleaned his teeth with the toothbrush he'd left at Freddy's during his stay in the winter. Remembering he'd lost one of his bags at the Café de Bore, he opened the drawer under his friend's bed and pulled out a tshirt to change into. Black seemed to be the "in" colour all year round here, and he felt like blending in today. He rolled it down over his pale, emaciated torso that contrasted with the brown of his lower arms and legs. With his notebook and Dictaphone in the shoulder bag, he wrapped the remaining half a gram of cocaine back up, put in his wallet, slid it in the back pocket of his faded chino shorts, slipped the Bretons on, then took the lift down to street level.

Emerging onto Rue de Bretagne in shades, he looked at himself in the reflection of Mmmozza, the Italian deli next door where he liked to take coffee when his favourite waitress, Francesca, was working. Although hardly a local, he seemed altogether more comfortable and at home in the 3rd Arrondisement, where there were fewer tourists, more contemporary art galleries and fashion boutiques. Around the corner was the Marche des Enfants Rouges, and a few Chinese traiteurs where you could eat cheap, although he still wasn't hungry.

The heat had made his feet expand and fit the shoes a little better, as they no longer slid or pinched quite as much, so at least he could walk normally now. Sitting by the southern entrance to Canal Saint-Martin with them swinging inches above the murky water, Lester went over some of the "luxury words" he kept in a plastic wallet. "Satrap," he mouthed to himself. "An underling or middle manager in a religious order."

It was just gone four when his phone rang from an unknown number. As promised, the woman revealed the address of the café she wanted to meet, a five-minute walk up the western side of the canal. He thanked her for choosing the shaded side of the street, but she told him that it was to make sure he was travelling against the flow of traffic. When he got there, she told him not to order anything, but go inside, take a glass of water and wait. There was a huge fan on the bar, blowing the thick, smoky air back out into the street where leisurely couples were cooling themselves down with small foamy beers. Lester stood in front of the roaring blades and blew the perspiration off his face, glugging water when the phone rang again. The voice confirmed that he was wearing some sort of colonial helmet, and he didn't attempt a joke this time. He should now leave that place, the woman said, and cross the bridge to the sunny side of the street. Don't worry, she would meet him indoors. But he must go slowly, stopping on the bridge for a couple of minutes so she could check he wasn't being trailed, before going to another location she had chosen because there was no mobile phone reception. She would meet him underground.

Descending the stairs sheepishly, he was temporarily blinded by the darkness of the rustic wine cave. Even with his shades off, somebody could have put a gun to his head and he wouldn't have seen them. Once his eyes adjusted, he saw a woman in a white chemise sitting at one of only three little tables in the cellar surrounded by racks of dusty bottles.

"Hello, Janice Remarque?"

"Lester Langway?"

He tiptoed towards her quickly, as though trying to get to his seat in the cinema without disturbing the film. He took the tote bag off his shoulder and reached across the table to shake her hand.

She was sitting demurely in a black pencil skirt and tights, smoking gauloises, and had the long, thin posture of a swan. "Pleased to meet you. My caution may have come across as paranoid, but I hope you will understand why soon."

"Not at all. I quite liked it."

"I'm pretty good at knowing what creates headlines," she said. "You're not going to hear every single thought that I have today. You're not recording this, are you?"

Lester showed her his Dictaphone, off.

"Good. This is strictly off the record."

XX

Janice Remarque was born in a communal apartment in Strasbourg during the 1968 uprising. "Guy Debord was always around our squat. My mother slept around with the leaders of the S.I. My father, of course, wasn't allowed to be furious."

Lester took a note, *Mother slept with leaders.*

"What was it Debord said," Lester flicked at the lighter. "The more a class claims not to exist, the more powerful it is?"

"I'm not sure what you mean, in relation to my thesis?"

"You were privileged, weren't you?"

"To some extent, yes. I had family friends who were professors, but then we also weren't allowed chocolate."

With such impeccable credentials, Janice was a confident, swinging student at the modern, vehemently left-wing Paris Diderot University in the industrial east of Paris. She was an extremely attractive blonde who wore baggy jumpers and had knots in her hair. He could see her as the centre of male attention in some "non-hierarchical" anarchist social centre. Her thesis was supervised by the acclaimed media theorist and member of the Communist Party, Pierre Berteaux. Its title? *Gérard Derenne: Philosopher of the Spectacle.* A newspaper columnist quipped that she effectively created a new academic subject: Gérard Studies.

For research, Janice stalked Gérard for over a year, attending every book signing, queued up to sit in the audience of his TV appearances.

"This was twenty years after his seismic appearance on *Text*," Janice said. The infamous French chat show had intellectuals argue with one another long into the night. On his screen debut, as the 23-year-old author of a single book, Gérard demonstrated his flamboyant sex appeal. Here was a renaissance action-man who had just got back from Afghanistan, where he had ridden camels, supplied ammunition and smoked opium with the Mujahedeen, all the while proclaiming that idea of left and right were redundant, and that Marxism was as dangerous a cult as Fascism. He screamed, ripped open his shirt and jumped on the coffee table to emphasise his passion for liberal, enlightenment and romantic ideas.

Like many serious readers of Philosophy, Janice had been unimpressed by Gérard's ideas as he disseminated them through books, then newspaper columns, TV shows and movies. Throughout her studies, she remained unwavering in her belief that France's new superstar philosopher was a spectacular bullshit artist, an intellectual poseur whose image was more powerful than his thought. Berteaux, her supervisor, believed she had written a thorough and theoretically sound critique, outlining the contradictions and intellectual shallowness of Gérard's positions, his frequent plagiarism, as well as analysing the increasingly cynical way he used his celebrity to manipulate public opinion.

A couple of months before her thesis was due to be handed in, she went against her supervisor's wishes by approaching Gérard for an interview, and was surprised to receive a positive response. "I contacted his agent, but he wrote back personally, giving me an unequivocal yes."

Janice tried to remain professional and critical as she waited in the anteroom of his lavish apartment on Boulevard Saint-Germain. She had been warned by plenty of her comrades that Gérard was not only a muppet, but a dangerous one. "Pierre implored me not to go. He reminded me how after he wrote a scathing review of Gérard's Marx biography, he frequently found himself sitting in front of Uri Geller on aeroplanes." Berteaux was convinced that Gérard had hired the Israeli psychic to control his mind. He also suspected that he sent female delegates to conferences—famous actresses and singers—to honeytrap him. But this only convinced Janice that her mentor, like so many on the left, had already lost his mind, and was determined to make up hers for herself.

"No matter your politics, to be in the orbit of somebody that powerful was very exciting," she said. "He insists to this day that it was just a coincidence, but he had scheduled our interview directly after a fireside chat with Bob Dylan."

"Dylan is like my second father."

"Mine too. I used to fantasise about hanging out with him in Greenwich Village. You know, if I was my parents' age, I think I would have done. Well, you can't turn back time, so this had to be the next best thing, right?"

Lester's chair screeched as he dragged it across the floor of the wine cave. Despite his first impressions about her upbringing, he found her to be refreshingly unpretentious and tender. "Did you meet Bob?"

"I sound like such a fangirl. I'll never forget it. As Dylan was leaving Gérard's study, he winked at me and said: 'Go easy on him, kiddo,'" Janice put on a husky voice. "'He says you got a mind like thunder.'"

"That really is despicably charming," Lester said.

"I wrote a song about it," she said. "Would you like to hear it?"

"Um, maybe later?"

"It's called 'The Ballad of Gérard Derenne'.

> *I was only twenty-four*
> *And defensive of my values*
> *You tore down my guard*
> *Like a Marxist-Leninist statue."*

Janice's fragile voice whistled around the cave. She seemed to have transported herself back into that time and place, staring ahead as if watching a replay on a screen. A single drop of mascara ran down her pallid cheek.

Lester went to the bathroom to top himself up with cocaine. When he came back with a bundle of tissues to give to her, Janice had composed herself and was ready to continue.

"What were your first impressions of Gérard?" he sniffed.

"A lot of people have said it, and I can tell you it really is true. He is the same as Bill Clinton..."

"He plays the saxophone?"

"No."

"He's a rapist?"

"Please stop interrupting! Let me tell you." Lester dug his fingers into the corner of his eyes when he was embarrassed. "When Gérard spoke, everyone in the room thought he was speaking *directly to them*."

"How many people were in the room when you met?"

"Two."

"Just you and him?"

"Yes."

"What did he do to you?"

"We reconsidered some key positions."

"Like what?"

"Hegel, Freud, Picasso, art in general. But mostly, about himself."

"So in a sense, Pierre was right to be suspicious."

"He had my journal articles printed out, had read them all in meticulous detail and made extensive notes. His insights were definitely not shallow, as I had assumed they would be. When I asked a tough question, he seemed to like it. He said he valued his critics as much as his friends; he often learned more from them. It was so refreshing to hear, after being surrounded by such insecure, petty arguments on the radical left, where certain ideas and principles are off-limits. He even gave me a bottle of vodka to give to his 'beloved rival,' Pierre. When I got home at 4am, Pierre was drunk, screaming about an intelligence sting operation to divide the far-left, an industrialist conspiracy to drive him insane. I told him I thought it was the drink and the self-loathing that drove him mad. That was the last time we spoke. Six months later, he was dead."

After their meeting, Gérard would call Janice and ask how he came across on TV and what he should write about for his next newspaper column. Within a few weeks of handing in her dissertation, she was accompanying him to Formula One races with Alain Delon and on other glamorous adventures. "I was poolside at Gérard's villa in Marrakesh one time. He was wearing just a towel, talking on one of those huge old mobile phones to the Minister of the Exterior, imploring him to intervene in the case of a young

French academic who had been sentenced to death in Iran. I sat on a sun lounger in my bikini, passing notes to Jean-Claude Van Damme, who was holidaying with us. He pledged to go undercover in Iran and break her out of jail."

"Did it work?"

"No, they hanged her before Jean-Claude even set off."

"It's the thought that counts," Lester said.

A couple came downstairs then and took one of the two other tables in the cellar. Janice gave them the once-over to check they weren't eavesdropping. The man was wearing a pair of ill-fitting flowered shorts and perspiring. When they made their orders in English, Janice seemed satisfied they were British ignoramuses who wouldn't understand a word she said, although she couldn't be too sure, so she and Lester hunkered closer together.

"Were you officially employed by Gérard at this time, or just a kind of... companion?"

"He put me on the payroll at the new company he'd set up to manage all his affairs under one roof, because he had become a business by this point."

"What was it called?"

"Humbert Humbert."

"After the main character in Lolita?"

"Yes. It worked as a codename. So whenever anybody asked, or if we were booking a hotel room and wanted to remain anonymous, we'd say we worked for Humbert Humbert. That usually shut people up."

"What was your job title?"

"With Gérard, job titles mean very little. As well as intelligence, he likes to surround himself with auras and energies."

Lester chomped on the end of his pen, then pointed it at her as if making a cold guess. "Isn't this just an airy-fairy way of saying he hires attractive young women?"

Janice drummed her slender fingers on the table and took a deep breath. "At this point, I have to clarify that I have signed an NDA that prevents me from disclosing any sensitive information. What I have told you so far is just my biography. I am happy to talk to you about my career in general terms, and I can guide you through the history of Gérard, but I'm not willing to go on the record."

"That's fine," Lester said, enjoying the cool of the wine cave and her company.

XXI

At 7pm, Lester knocked back a cup of mouthwash and gargled. Checking himself out in the big cosmetic mirror, the rosé sun kissed the apartments in Montmartre and the leaves of the linden trees dappled his skin with delicate penumbra. His cheeks were becoming hollow and more pronounced by stubble. Not bad at all, he thought to himself, rolling women's deodorant under his armpits. He certainly wouldn't mind taking a bubble bath before drifting into a deep sleep. Replacing the scented stick in the bathroom cabinet, he rummaged through the many devices, cosmetics, creams and pills stored away in there. The epilator, that's a good omen, he thought. The tube of haemorrhoid cream caused slight alarm, as did the box labelled "lithium". He was good to go until he noticed that he'd put Freddy's t-shirt on inside-out.

Before he'd even turned it around, there was something about the way it felt that made him a little uneasy, like he knew, subconsciously, what was printed on the other side. Turning it over, he saw that it was the gift he had given to Freddy as a thank-you for letting him stay for a week in December. Of course, his friend, the politically incorrect comedian, had appreciated it, but he wasn't sure it would play well with a sophisticated, professional woman who described herself as a second-wave feminist. Luckily, he had in his contacts the number of the world's leading expert on the matter.

"Shawn, it's Lester Langway from *Down N Out!* magazine," Lester said into his phone, hoping he couldn't be heard in the room next door. "We met at the Pornhub conference in November. How are you?"

"Hey, man, I'm good thanks," Shawn said in a laid-back American drawl. "I never received that copy of the magazine you said you'd send me, but that's okay."

"I am so sorry. I will email the office as soon as I get off the line."

"Don't worry about it. What can I do for you?"

"As you know, I'm a huge fan of your work. Along with Ron

Jeremy, I think you're one of the most underappreciated underground actors of our time. In fact, I'm wearing your tshirt as we speak."

"The Milf Hunter one?"

"Yeah." Lester made a horrified face at himself in the mirror.

"That's good to hear, man. Where are you?"

"Paris."

"Awesome, I love French Milfs, they're unlike any other."

"You said if I ever needed advice, I could call you, so that's what I'm doing."

"Um, sure, what's the problem? Is it to do with hunting Milfs?"

"It is, kind of," Lester cringed, wiped the sweat from beneath his khaki helmet. "I'm actually in a French woman's house, and I think there might be a chance of me staying the night, or maybe even longer. It's a really, really nice place, and she's... let's just say she's a very valuable source for the story I'm writing."

"Ooookay, I think I get where you're coming from."

"The trouble is, I just want to sleep here. How do you think I should play it?"

"You want to know how *not* to fuck a Milf? That's a new one for the Milf Hunter."

"I appreciate that."

"Is there not a couch you can sleep on?"

"There is, but it's really uncomfortable."

"It seems to me like you should maybe explain the situation, say you've been working hard, you're really tired, but you're not busy tomorrow morning, wink-wink, know what I'm saying?"

"I hear you, that makes a lot of sense."

"Then if you still don't feel like it, in the morning you can just leave."

"I hear you. That would be poor Milf Hunting etiquette though, surely?"

"I don't know, man." Impatience was creeping into Shawn's voice. Pounding music with a 4/4 beat was playing in the background. "If you're not trying to fuck her, what you're doing isn't technically Milf Hunting. It's something else."

"True, true."

"Listen, man I gotta go, we're opening up here already."

"Oh yeah, you on a shoot?"

"I quit the adult industry, man. Opened a bar in Fort Lauderdale, Florida. Hunter's Bar, it's called, right on the beach. If you're ever in town, drop in for a cold one."

"Will do," Lester said. "Thank you, Mr Hunter."

XXII

"What would you say is the highlight of your life, Janice?" Lester was lying on the chaise-lounge with his shoes off, blowing smoke out of the French windows that opened onto a small hillside vineyard, surrounded by sun-smattered white buildings with terraces and turrets.

"Probably co-directing *Gérard & Jacques*." Janice was sitting on a rug with her feet pressed together, some kind of yoga pose. "Have you seen it?"

"No, and to be honest, I don't think I'm in the mood to watch a film."

"I have seen it too many times already. But if you like cinema verité, I think you will like it. There is an extremely tense scene in Aleppo."

"You went to Syria—was it during the conflict?"

"Yes. When Gérard and Jacques arrived, the city was predicted to fall to Assad's forces in less than forty-eight hours without reinforcements. We were driving through the night so they could deliver night-vision goggles to the rebels when our Hummer broke down. Instead of calling the US military to come and rescue them, Gérard and Jacques set off walking twenty miles across the desert, Gérard with his white scarf over his head, Jacques with a Palestinian keffiyeh, rocket launchers over their shoulders."

"And... did they make it?"

"Their path was blocked by an American army tank. They were detained for seventy-two hours, then released when the city had already fallen."

"Were they tortured?"

"No."

"That's a shame," Lester said.

"Would you like to see the night-vision goggles?"

"You have a pair? Sure."

Janice came back with a pair of bulky goggles with a large square interface. Lester pinged the strap against his head and felt instantly disoriented. The room was upside down, and when he got up to move around, objects staggered and fragmented, as if he was on ketamine.

"They were designed by the artist Ludwig Munch," Janice said.

"What use would they be in a warzone?" Lester banged his shin on the coffee table and grunted. "Ah!"

"Are you okay?"

Rubbing his bare leg, "I'm fine."

"Poor thing. Gérard said he wanted to turn the world upside down. He chose an artist to make the goggles because he believes that artists and writers are society's true leaders, and their weapons are more powerful than bombs."

"Thank god he didn't make it to the rebels. They'd have stumbled into enemy fire."

"Maybe that's true. But like you say, it's the thought that counts. And besides, they look great on film. Here, do you mind if I take a picture of you?"

"As long as you don't post it anywhere."

"Of course not. Nobody will know you've been here."

"Are you sure? You seemed pretty convinced we were being watched."

"If we are, we are. There's nothing in my NDA that prevents me from having a writer over to my house."

She tapped her phone and giggled. Then Janice came over to him and sat on the end of the chaise-lounge. "What's the highlight of *your* short life so far?"

The cocaine was no longer getting him high, just keeping him awake. He forced himself up into a semi-sitting position, eyes peeling open. "This assignment, if all goes well."

"And how is it going so far?"

"In this beautiful apartment, in my favourite city, it's going very nicely. I wish I could stay longer."

"That's very sweet of you. You know, I'm really glad you contacted me. It's good talking to you."

"Really, in what way?"

"I've met so many journalists, but you're different somehow. Every editor and all the best writers in France have been into the Surrealist Central. I showed them around myself, introduced them to the women, wined them, dined them, gave them unreleased snippets of films and manuscripts. We had Johnny Hallyday and Sasha Distel come in to give private concerts for them. I don't suppose you've heard about the ESCHATON office? It's a legendary place. Even the NDAs are infamous in the art world."

"Actually, I swung by there yesterday. Purely by chance."

"Really? Did the women on the front desk scare you?"

"Just a bit."

"Ah, yes, that's all part of the game. You know, it's a place that exists outside of conventional time and space. Upstairs there's a cinema, a theatre, a collection of original paintings by Ernst, de Chrico, the diamond-encrusted tortoise that belonged to Huysmans, a hundred and fifty years old! There's even a replica of the Café de Cyrano, where the Surrealists used to have their meetings."

"They wouldn't let me in," Lester sighed. "I'd love to go."

"I still have visiting privileges, but after what you say happened last night, there's no way I could get you back in, you'll be blacklisted."

"It's okay, I'm used to working from the outside. But what's Gérard's obsession with the Surrealists? It seems to me like they'd have had a field day with him if they had ever crossed paths."

"People on the outside, who only read the smears or the celebrity gossip, misunderstand him. Gérard regards himself as an outsider, a dissident, who still doesn't belong in the establishment. In his mind, he is still the *enfant terrible* of French letters. Every year he refuses the Legion d'Honneur, because he says a writer's place is as an emissary between society and the abyss."

"I might be inclined to agree with him."

"Gérard used to say that Paris in the twenties was an *intellectual coliseum*. In the late twenties Robert Desnos, the savant of the Surrealists, was excommunicated, along with Bataille and others in the *Second Manifesto of Surrealism*. With the writing no longer working out, Desnos decided to open a nightclub in Montparnasse called Maldoror, after the text by Lautréamont. When they found out, Breton, Aragon and a couple of Surrealist heavies stormed the place and smashed it up. All over the naming of a bar! That's the length they were willing to go to protect a text. Gérard loves that story, he says it is the example he expects his employees to follow to protect him and his ideas."

"I have to say, part of me admires it."

"Just like Breton, he had his daily meetings, where he would remind us who our enemies were. As soon as a negative article came out, he would dispatch one of the women to go and speak to the editor, remind them we could have their advertising pulled, their taxes investigated. But his worst spleen was reserved for women who left on bad terms, who threatened legal action against him. If they wouldn't take his money, then things got... out of hand, sometimes."

By the way she circled her finger on the upholstery, he could tell that Janice was taking steps down the path towards his confidence.

"Out of hand in what way?"

"Gérard used private investigators and other... individuals... to follow people, make sure they weren't considering going public with their grievances."

"Interesting, what kind of grievances?"

Janice looked out of the window, into the distance.

"Who are these women, Janice? Do you have their names?"

Her hand appeared on his leg then, and it felt good.

"Are you going to tell me why you left?"

Janice's fingers crawled up his leg, tingly. "Let's stop talking about him, shall we? I want to get to know *you*."

He clenched her hand to stop her from going any further.

She had mounted him. He was lying back on the chaise-lounge, unsure of how to get out of this compromising situation. The thought of a camera in the ceiling gave him shudders. Janice tugged at his shirt. "Why don't you take this off? I can give you a massage."

"No! I mean, yes. But only if I can remain fully clothed."

XXIII

Lester was perched on the edge of the chaise-lounge, enjoying the deep, sensual relief of Janice working his shoulders and back. At his request, they stopped listening to Gérard's album, *Monsieur Amour*, and played 'Ce Mortel Ennuie' by Alain Goraguer. Janice was down to just her bra.

"Mmm, that's good."

"There? You have a couple of knots in your back."

"Mmm-hmm." As he moved his eyes around her exquisite apartment, he couldn't help but wonder what kind of deal she might have with Gérard. "I hear it's difficult to fire workers in France."

"Almost impossible unless they have robbed or killed somebody."

"Even if they go through the correct procedure, there's a chance they will get dragged through the courts, where sensitive information may come to light. Am I right?"

"You're on the right track."

"Hypothetically speaking, some companies are better off keeping difficult employees on the payroll, putting them on gardening leave, and keeping a close eye on them."

"Gardening leave? I don't have a garden. Only pot plants."

"It's an English expression. It means paid to keep your mouth shut."

"That's so cynical. France has an extremely fair balance between workers' and bosses' interests. Gérard even helped draft the legislation with the Minister of the Interior, who is a personal friend."

"So you're still technically employed by him, am I right?"

"I don't need to go to work in the morning, if that's what you mean."

Lester was feeling very light-headed. When he saw Janice's huge white bedroom with blackout curtains and air conditioning, he thought he'd entered a dream—a dream of spies. He flopped onto the bed face down, arms and legs spready-outy. Janice went into her ensuite to brush her teeth. When she came back, she was naked, but

Lester didn't even notice. "Aww, you don't want to go to sleep yet, do you?" she asked, stroking his hair.

"I can't keep my eyes open," he groaned. "I'll be much more lively in the morning. I don't have to start work early. I'll cook you a full English breakfast. But first, I got to sleep."

"Okay, as you please."

He drifted off with all the thoughts turned down to one percent in his mind, and then click, he was gone.

XXIV

He woke with a stabbing headache, mouth like the bottom of a bird's cage and terrible hunger. The shapes in darkness were unfamiliar. He couldn't recall who this woman beside him was, or how he'd got there. Despite wanting to drop back into the black hole, he desperately needed to pee, so he threw the covers off and staggered into the bathroom. The time was just past midnight. His phone had a message from Anaïs, asking what he was up to. He wondered that himself. He couldn't remember half of what had gone on yesterday, but was convinced he must have embarrassed himself somehow. He couldn't stand the idea of being here in the morning and having to talk to her, that was for sure.

Out on the street, he looked both ways before sprinting into the Métro with images of a young Alain Delon trailed by the cops in Jean-Pierre Melville's *Le Samouraï* reeling through his projector at twice the speed. Should he take a circular route, get out a couple of stops before his station, or did they know already from Uri Geller's mind-readings that he was heading to the Deadbeat Hotel?

On the Métro, with his phone about to die, he texted Anaïs: "How did your date go?"

"Not bad," she replied.

"Where are you now?"

"About to leave. What are you up to?"

"Going to the Deadbeat to sleep."

"What's the Deadbeat?"

"Deadbeat Hotel. A friend's place."

"I didn't think you had any friends."

"I barely know this guy."

"Can I come?"

"Sure."

Anaïs arrived at the Deadbeat Hotel on Rue Saint-Lazare shortly after Lester. He and the apartment's owner, Luke Mayakovsky, were sitting on rocking horses in his minimalist living room, trying to remember how he had met this hospitable Australian redneck with the mullet who worked for the fashion designer Rick Owens. At Stolly's bar two years ago, they concluded. Lester had written him a poem on a napkin.

"Fancy a beer?"

"It couldn't make me feel any worse." That was inaccurate. It made him feel dizzy and nauseous.

"And what brings you to Paris?" Mayakovsky asked.

"Trying to secure an interview with Gérard Derenne for *Down N Out!* magazine."

"Ah, that guy. He asked Rick to design some uniforms for his staff a while back. But he declined. Rick's always talking about how much he hates this guy."

Then another Aussie voice came from the bedroom:

"Luke!"

"What is it, Carlo? I've got guests."

"Who's that?"

"Carlo."

"Is that your, uh, boyfriend?"

"No."

"Okay." Lester stuck his head out of the window to try and cool down, then inspected the apartment. There were a few carefully placed books by cult authors that Mayakovsky hadn't read on the shelves, and a large collection of fashion magazines, including the last five years' worth of *Down N Out!*

"Is that my bed?"

"Yeah."

"It looks like a coffin."

"It's one of Rick's coffins."

"Great! Can I try it out?" Anaïs said.

"Go ahead. It's one of seven Rick had made. He gave them to the people who work for him. He told us we can keep them until he decides to die."

"Decides to die... you mean, he's going to..."

"Yeah."

"Has he decided how?"
"Fucked to death by a horse."
"Has he chosen the horse yet?"
"No."
"We should run a sweepstake."
"Good idea," Mayakovsky said. "Anyway, I'm going to bed. Got to be up early to go to work. I'll text you to let you know if your package arrives."

Lester knew he was going to enjoy abusing this guy's hospitality.

As for the girl, Lester had come to adopt what Mushroom Daley had called an "ultra-receptive posture," a way of beckoning chance. He had left his mind open in the hope of finally waking beside a companion, and yet this is who he ended up with? This poor Catholic *gamine* who bundled around Paris in constant graveyard mode, apathetic to the core but sweet as sin. She lay in the coffin with her lips puckered.

After a few minutes, when she didn't feel him beside her, she asked, "Lester, what are you doing? Are you coming to death? Sorry, I mean bed."

"Standing by the window, smoking, thinking."

"Thinking about what?"

"Oh, just this case." Then he realised, when you start looking for Gérard, you see him everywhere. Locating him would be the journalistic equivalent of splitting atoms. "Tell me about something else. How did your date with Julien Badbeger go?"

"He took me to a billiard hall."

"Oh yeah?"

"He asks if he can sleep with you if he wins."

"Did you win?"

"Of course I won."

"Did you ask him anything about Gérard, or say anything about me?"

"No."

"Can you give me his number?"

"Sure, although I'm not sure if he's into guys."

He took his shoes and socks off, even his shorts and shirt, and vaulted on top of the black catafalque. There was room for two if they pressed up against one another. At the moment when he was expecting a touch on the leg or shoulder, perhaps to warn it off out of fear of his own imperfections, he mentioned work: "I think we should make some posters."

"What kind?"

" 'Wanted' posters."

"Nobody makes 'Wanted' posters anymore."

"Exactly. That's why we're going to do it."

WEDNESDAY

XXV

It was only 8am but Fashion Week waited for no man. Mayakovsky came into the living room of the Deadbeat Hotel with two coffees he'd spent fifteen minutes aero-pressing, and two of the finest croissants from Rue des Martyrs, for his guests. Anaïs was still asleep on her back like a corpse. Lester, who'd sweated profusely into the padded coffin, popped a couple of cocodamols and his antidepressant and pawed at the coffee cup.

"So Lester," Mayakovsky said. "You should listen to this dream I had."

Lester grabbed the Breton biography, staggered through the corridor, sat on the dumper, listened to Mayakovsky describe his dream. "For some strange reason, there was a new rule implemented in the football World Cup, where every team had to select a cultural representative in their squad. And you, yeah, you of all people, were the English cultural representative. For England this was actually quite a good rule, because they had plenty to choose from, but it effectively disqualified Italy when they realised they have no modern culture. Anyway, you weren't expected to get a kick, but due to injuries, you came onto the pitch and did better than anyone expected. Then Arsenal signed you, and it made me real jealous because every time I'd go to see them play, you would be playing for them."

"That's a... really sweet dream." Lester flushed the bog.

"So," back in the corridor, Mayakovsky asked, "did you bang her?"

Lester might have still been drunk. He claimed that he had turned his timidity into superior will, boasting, "I profoundly surprised her by denying the omnipotence of her charm and I exposed her weakness in the dead of night."

The shower was splattered with bloodstains left by the last guests to pass by the Deadbeat, a New Zealand biker gang. Scurrying across the chipped tiles with wet feet and a miniature towel wrapped around his middle, Lester searched the apartment for a shirt he could change into while Mayakoksky did some stretching and head-banging to Champagne Holocaust, a South London band Lester had discovered. The weather on his phone told him it was going to be another scorcher, so shorts were definitely in order, as was something in addition to his colonial helmet to rebound the psychic rays that might be beamed at him.

"Why are you wearing my England football shirt?" Mayakovsky asked.

"I like to dress in other people's dreams," he said, squirting himself with Lynx Africa from his Chanel bottle. His shirt was the Euro '96 one worn by wayward genius Paul Gascoigne. Lester had tracked down the swollen-faced alcoholic to his bedsit in Grimsby to conduct a sympathetic interview. He'd arrived brandishing a bottle of gin as an incentive, and left six hours later with a cut above his eye and a broken Dictaphone.

The music woke Anaïs, who made a cat noise. Lester tore off pieces of croissant and waved them at her. She bit them out of his hand, nodding her head in appreciation as she chewed them and sniffed out the coffee without opening her eyes.

Part of him wanted to hide away and sleep some more, but he was anxious to check his emails and social media accounts, so he grabbed Mayakovsky's laptop. Nobody at *Down N Out!* had got in contact to tell him Gérard had called to ask for him and therefore the job was back on. The folks at ESCHATON productions, the former editors of Editions Derenne, newspapers and TV stations had all ignored his follow-up emails.

Now the booze and drugs were evacuating his system, he was ashamed of his behaviour at Café de Bore and the aftermath. He didn't know how he was going to get through the rest of the day, let alone the week. No more drinking, that's for sure.

While he was hunched over the laptop, a familiar-looking man emerged in his underwear, rubbing his eyes—an occupational hazard of not having an office.

"Hey, Carlo, meet Lester Langway from *Down N Out!* magazine."

Soft, dreamy codeine blurred the edges of his thoughts now.

"No way," Carlo said. "I was going to message you, but I didn't take your card. Can I have those shoes back?"

"Um, sure, here you go." Lester located them by smell alone, besides the catafalque, and handed them back.

"No, those aren't the ones. Mine were black, they had a pointy toe."

"Huh?" It seemed Carlo was right. These were dark brown, more like his desert boots with a roundish toe.

"I swear these are the ones I took from you. Look here, it says 'Breton' on the sole."

"Sure, I believe you," Carlo smiled. "To be honest, I wasn't mad on them, so I'll let you off. But there was something inside. I'm going to a party tonight. I'm broke and I can't turn up without it."

Lester grimaced. "I'll sort it out for you later today, as soon as I get paid."

He slipped the shoes on. They fit way better than when he'd first acquired them, like they were moulding themselves to his feet. And they looked much more fitting with his faded chino shorts and colonial helmet.

XXVI

Codeine was like a warm bath in his veins. When that no longer eased the pain, he'd get somebody to lob a toaster in. Working on it wasn't always easy, however. It made him drowsy and prone to reminiscence, so he spent a couple of hours scanning social media looking for former employees of ESCHATON Productions and Humbert Humbert. They weren't the kind of places you advertised a former employment at. You either moved straight into another top job with a stellar recommendation, or you vanished. Although his open-source research skills were so unsophisticated—they didn't extend far beyond Google.

At ten he woke Anaïs. She had flakes of sleep in her eyes, zapped of energy, but comfortable in her little dead zone. He sprinkled his fingers under the arms, down her sides. "Tickle, tickle, tickle! Time to get up!"

"Tickling doesn't work if you were beaten as a child."

"Oof. Alright. What's your plan?"

"I'll get up soon."

"Aren't you supposed to go to work today?"

"I can't be bothered."

"Suits me. What about the posters?"

"Tell me what you want on them."

"A photo of Gérard. 'Wanted: Dead or Alive. Any information call—.' My phone number. We'll paste them around Saint-Germain tomorrow. Do you think you'll be able to design it by then?"

"I'll have to go home to use my laptop."

Now he was leaving, he wished he could lie back down with her there, or even better, retire to a private room with a locked door and no deadline. But he couldn't, because he had the mystery of missing philosophers to solve and an overdraft to replenish.

Before he left, he slipped on his special shades with rear-view mirrors on the wings. Acquired during a successful tug-of-war with his grandmother over a Christmas cracker, he tried to read the names of mailboxes downstairs. Just about could do. Out the door, he took a couple of false turns, went into the Métro at Cadet then came back out again. There was nothing happening in the rearview mirror except the usual crowds in designer sunglasses talking on phones against a backdrop of white facades, crenelated rooftops and churches. Even that disappointed him. He reminded himself that he wasn't angry with the world, just hungry. But on Rue du Faubourg Montmarte, a gauntlet of gourmets were gobbling giblets. His guts were gonging like gunshots. In a greengrocer he grabbed a golden apple. Gnashing and gnarling at a grandmother getting grapefruits, gambooges, genips, gelia melons and gak fruit—"Getonwithit!" he screamed under his breath. He spent his last sixty-five cents on a peach and crossed his fingers that his package had arrived at Mayakovsky's work.

On Boulevard Haussmann, he saluted the Rex theatre, a red and white art deco palace from better times. With juice from the peach running down his chin and his stomach still empty, tears appeared in his eyes. He wished he could have witnessed the New Wave of cinema wash through Europe, and been around when an outsider like Belmondo's characters could at least afford a seedy hotel room. He cursed being alive now, when culture was dead and journalism no longer paid a living wage. He wondered how the hell a lad his age, who was barely more than a student, was expected to do the job without a secretary, an office, a salary or even a bed to sleep in. The only consolation was that unlike Tom Perkins, rewriting agency copy in North Wales, he could work on his own time, pounding the pavements of Paris, and at least pretend to be a proper reporter. Because like Breton, he too had the desire to magnify individual experience into something that joined with the flow of marvels running, like a magic subway, under the monotonous pavement of daily existence. Although it was hard to appreciate when you were glued to your smartphone, refreshing news feeds every five minutes for a mention of the missing Gérard…

There had been no updates. The most recent entry was the same story he'd read dozens of times, a short news item by the Associated

Press six months ago, shortly after his farewell newspaper column, noting that Gérard had abandoned his "troops" for parts unknown. " 'I'm going without my phone or leaving an address,' he'd told one of his friends. And with no hope of return[...] All those who counted on him are starting to understand that he's far from being a leader, only a tyrant."

Lester slumped on a bench outside the Pompidou Centre and scanned through the copy of Andrew Marr's *My Trade* that he often turned to for guidance—a hand on the shoulder from a father of British journalism. He underlined and then copied out phrases as they resonated, based on no general sense other than the aesthetic or emotional.

> Volunteer exiles. A more precarious and interesting life. The similarities between drugs and news don't stop there. As they eat, news can brighten their faces. Eyewitness accounts. Police intelligence. Fashionable world. Editor told him to use his fucking imagination. High literature this was not. The first question is to ask, who benefits from publishing this? Who is damaged? The booze does not always work in the journalist's interests. Stories can be stolen.

Looking at it through the eyes of a veteran newspaper editor and journalist, he sensed that a big story would break, but now the excitement of the party had worn off and he was essentially vagrant, he didn't stand much chance, realistically, of being the one to do it. With no contacts nor experience in tracking down missing persons, this trip had been a massive overestimation of his ability.

But then, as Andrew Marr reminded him, the reporter on more than ninety percent of the world's newspapers is merely a creature of routine, an automaton.

He picked himself up and used a Métro ticket to get to the Sorbonne.

XXVII

It was mid-June, the end of the academic year. Students were in a cheerful, elevated mood, hugging and kissing one another. He couldn't believe it was more than two years since he'd picked up his grades and celebrated his first-class honours degree in Political Science by taking a tab of LSD on his own in the park.

In the Sorbonne Philosophy department, young intellectuals with geeky backpacks were queuing up to receive envelopes with their tickets to a brighter future. "Excuse me," he said to a kid at the back of the line. "Do you know Jacques Dutronc?"

The lanky young man smiled. He had salad between his teeth and mayonnaise in his stubble. "I was in his third-year seminar."

"Really?" taking out notepad... "What was it on?"

"Immanuel Kant. Professor Dutronc is the world's leading expert on the moral imperative. It was such an honour."

"That makes sense. When was the last time you met with him?"

"Last week, he invited students for aperitifs in his office."

"That's odd," Lester said. "When I called the office, they said he no longer worked here. Was he..."

"That's right, he doesn't work here anymore. He's retired."

"Great, thank you!" Lester felt like hugging the kid. There would be no need to go and harass the administrators, whose refusal to answer simple questions would drive him round the bend. "I don't suppose he said where he was going?"

"Yes, but I can't remember, sorry."

"Did he mention anything at all about Gérard?"

"Yes, he was always talking about him, they're best friends."

The kid got to the front of the line and received his envelope. "Yes!" He jumped up and punched the air, pure goof. "An A! Now I can start my internship at the World Bank."

"Congratulations!" Lester almost kissed him. "What are you doing after this? Would you like to go for a drink? I have an expense account waiting to be abused by a fellow like you."

"Sure! I'll see you at the Café de Bore. My classmates are already there. Look for two young radicals in berets smoking."

Lester wished there were more people in the world like Walter Fedelman. He didn't waste time hooking up with Dutronc's students, hands twitching with excitement as he ripped through the journalistic textbook, with his legs following.

As a general rule of thumb, Lester had learned that it was best to wait three days before returning to the scene of drunken embarrassment. By that point, the manager was usually willing to write it all off as an old war story. Barely forty-eight hours had passed, but it felt like he'd been in Paris for months already. Aware that his England football shirt and colonial helmet might have been a poor sartorial choice for Boulevard Saint-Germain, he still walked through the decorative shrubs of the Bore with his shoulders back, projecting an image of sophisticated composure. Like a true English colonist, he belonged anywhere and everywhere. On the crowded corner terrace, he spotted two kids wearing berets and denim jackets with Baader-Meinhof pin badges, rolling cigarettes, and introduced himself.

"Are you by any chance Jacques Dutronc's students?"

"We sure are, monsieur. We couldn't very well lie about it, could we?"

"I guess not." He shouldn't drink. But his hands were shaking, and besides, everyone else on the terrace seemed to be enjoying theirs without any trouble. "One small beer please," he told the waiter. To celebrate the breakthrough. "Make room for Walter, shall I?"

"No," the boy said. "She's going straight home to Geneva after class."

"But he said..."

"Don't listen to what she says," the girl said. "*She's* a pathological liar."

"Oh yeah?"

"She identifies as a she."

"Does she look like a *she* to you?"

"She's not a Philosophy student."

"She's not even at the Sorbonne."

"Yeah, they sent her here on an *empowerment programme*."

"An empowerment programme for pathological liars."

"What?" Lester could sense the net widening again. "But he—sorry, she—told me you were here, and that turned out to be true."

"Even a broken clock is right twice a day."

They were cute, these two. He could imagine sharing a squat with them and composing pamphlets together.

"Look," the boy leaned in, "we're not supposed to tell anybody this, but shit's getting really fucked up in academia right now."

"They're rewriting the most fundamental philosophical concepts."

"What was it Orwell said, two-plus-two equals five?"

"Wait, wait, hold on a minute." Lester took a big glug of beer and tore through his notepad to a clean page. "What, exactly, is going on? Let's start with specific facts, people and events."

"They're using us as guinea pigs."

"Guinea pigs for what?"

"Don't have nightmares," the kid shrugged nonchalantly. "What you're seeing is just political enantiodromia."

"Sorry, what?"

"ENANTIODROMIA."

Lester tried to get the whole word down on paper.

"Carl Jung borrowed the concept of enantiodromia from Heraclitus. It's the principle that governs all cycles of natural life. Everything that exists turns into its *opposite*."

"So you know our beloved, 'Liberté, égalité, fraternité?' Turn them around and what do they become?"

Lester did the linguistic manoeuvre in his head, but the girl beat him to it. "Slavery, hierarchy, conflict."

"Catchy," Lester said morosely. "And where does Walter come into this?"

"Don't quote us on this, we don't want to be in your article," the boy said, "but we think she's a plant."

"A cactus?"

"Not that type of plant."

"A useful idiot."

"More than that."
"An agent of conflict."
"An unstable element.".
"Every class has one, doesn't it?" Lester said.
"You don't have to believe us if you don't want to."
"We're only undergraduates."
"No, please, I'm listening."
"Think about it."
"Why do you think they're infiltrating our class with a pathological liar?"
"Not just any class."
"And not just any philosophy class."
"A seminar on Kant? Please!"
"We're a pretty good litmus test, aren't we?"
"Litmus test for what?"
"Einstein said if World War III is fought with nuclear weapons, World War IV will be fought with sticks and stones."
"But that's not quite correct."
"World War III has already begun."
"It's not one empire against another."
"And it's not being fought with nuclear weapons, it's being fought with information."
"Language."
"Definitions."
"Facts."
"Pronouns."

Lester was just about following. He had to reel it back to tangibles. What would Andrew Marr ask? Who benefits? "Who planted him—sorry, her—in your class?"

"That's the million-euro question."
"Who runs this empowerment programme?" Lester asked.
"*So-called* empowerment programme."
"He said he's on a scholarship from the Fabian Society."
"But of course, we don't believe him."
"And that's the whole point."

"So you're saying, somebody's starting an information war," Lester said, "using Kantian philosophy as the battleground?"

"That's what Dutronc says, and we believe him."

"The categorical imperative is that you should always tell the truth."

"That's why they fired him."

"What?" Lester said. "I thought Dutronc was untouchable."

"So did he."

"So did we."

"But he refused to call Walter 'she', and Walter complained, so they fired him."

"Or rather, he took his retirement."

"I bet you're already questioning your own sanity, aren't you?"

On the contrary, he thought the world might be mad, but he was still just about sane. Now he understood why Dutronc was clearing out his office when they'd met, and why he seemed in such a sour mood. This ought to have been a story in its own right. He made a note to pitch an article about it to somebody.

"That's really helpful, thank you. Here's my number, if you think of anything else." Lester gave it to the girl and threw a few coins on the plate.

"See you later, comrade. We can't wait to read your article."

XXVIII

On his way to the Rick Owens office at the former Communist Party headquarters in Place du Palais-Bourbon, Lester passed by a school building engraved with the ominous motto, "Liberté, égalité, fraternité," and was reminded of Abraham Bosse's 1651 front-cover etching for Hobbes' *Leviathan*, showing the godlike king, prepared for war with a sword and crosier. In his strength, the leader literally embodied the feeble, frightened masses, from the serfs up to the clergymen. The idea that World War III might have already begun with a hair-splitting contest made him shudder.

While he waited for Mayakovsky to come down for his lunch break, he retreated to the shade and made a phone call to distract himself from anxious thoughts about the distant and imminent future.

"Hello, Tom Perkins, Western Rural News."

"Hello, Mr Perkins, I've got a story for you…"

"What is it, Les?"

"I'm looking for information about the Fabian Society. Presumably it's French, although it could also be Belgian, Canadian or Swiss."

"I'd love to help you, but I really have got to go. Somebody left a gate open overnight. Some sheep really have gone missing."

The owner of the city's cheapest hotel arrived, as he did everywhere, in a leather jacket, with a bottle of Heineken glued to his hand and a look of withered charm. He was also carrying a narrow cardboard package—a huge relief. Lester clinked the Heineken he'd shoplifted along the way against his pal's.

"What's in this?" Mayakovsky shook the package.

"Do you like speed? Shrooms? Acid? MDMA? DMT? 2CB?"

"I'm partial." Mayakovsky sniffed, wiped his bogey finger on the white tshirt he never took off. "Some guy tried to collect it earlier. I had to tell him to fuck off."

"What? Who did he say he was?"

Mayakovsky read the name on the package. "He said his name

was Jacques Vaché."

"That's really weird."

"I thought so too. Where did you get that name from?"

"Jacques Vaché was Breton's best friend. They exchanged letters from the trenches. Breton claimed they were the inspiration for Surrealism."

"Hmm, well this guy had a military haircut and a passport that said he was Jacques Vaché."

"You're joking, right?"

"Nah. There's a pissed-off soldier looking for you now because you've got his drugs."

"Are you sure you haven't taken any of that stuff?"

"Positive."

"Alright, I need to open the package and give you something."

"Thanks, man."

Lester ripped it open with his keys and tore apart the silver vacuum pack. Inside were an assortment of pills, baggies full of white powders and natural supplements. In the doorway, they did a bump of speed off a key and wrapped the little mound into a receipt.

"Give this to Carlo for the other night."

"Oh yeah," Mayakovsky sniffed. "He told me you were at the same party. That's another weird coincidence."

"He designed some shoes for Gérard, didn't he?"

"I don't remember him saying anything about that. But then, I don't really take much interest in him. He just sleeps in my bed."

"He said he works for Berluti."

"He said that? I don't think Carlo works for Berluti. He doesn't have a job, he's a freelance consultant. Or should I say, unemployed."

"Weird, he told me he was head of the footwear division."

"Don't trust him, he's a compulsive liar."

Not another one, Lester thought. He sold the rest of the "85 percent pure cocaine" to Mayakovsky and stuffed his wallet with 350 euros.

XXIX

Earlier that morning, Lester had texted Julien Badbeger and asked for a date. Without revealing who he was—just an "admirer from England"—he was hoping to ambush him. As he was perusing the book stalls along the bank of the Seine, the novelist texted back: "3pm, Belleville billiard hall. Winner takes all?"

"See you there," Lester replied. "Bring your wallet."

Even with the key of wet, fishy amphetamine clogging his nostril, he didn't have the energy to walk all the way to Belleville in the northeast of the city. Wallet full, he no longer felt obliged to ration his Métro usage, so he arrived in the eastern quarter rested and prepared for the most important billiard game of his life.

The trashy pool hall was empty, splashed with neon adverts for cheap beer and phone numbers for prostitutes in the toilets. There was no security on duty at this hour, and there would be no doping committee to check for performance-enhancing drugs, either, so Lester swallowed a few flakes of speed and knocked them back with his pint of Desperado's. Having paid for an hour, he selected the straightest cue he could find, took the tray of balls and practised his game on one of the empty tables, lining up canons and plants underneath the spotlights before his opponent arrived.

Badbeger strode in at a quarter past the hour with a confrontational demeanour. He was short and brawny, a kind of corduroy caveman who wasted no time sizing Lester up.

"Are you here to get spanked?" He had a crazy-eye thing going on and spat when he talked.

"Hold on," Lester said. "Let's be clear about the rules."

"I win, you bend over. You win, I bend over. Shall we play? One-frame shootout?"

"I propose a slight modification."

Badbegar flicked the hair out of his eyes with a grimace. "Go ahead, let's hear it."

"If I win, you answer some questions."

"It's a deal," Badbeger said and racked them up.

The Frenchman won the coin toss and screwed through the balls, sinking one but missing his next shot. With the amphetamines coursing through his bloodstream, Lester felt as lucid as Ronnie O'Sullivan. He chalked his cue, crouched into position and didn't so much hit as stroke the white ivory globe across the cloth, caroming into his red at a 45-degree angle. If they were watching, Abraham Maslow and John Virgo both would have agreed that it was a "peak moment" as the red dropped into the middle of the cup, and the white bounced off two cushions, returning into a comfortable position in the middle of the table. Lester tapped a couple more in, raising his eyes before the ball had dropped to see Badbeger glugging his pint, clearly rattled. "Your turn." Badbeger had three options with the white parked against the baulk cushion: attempt a low-percentage long pot into the bottom corner; roll up behind for a snooker; hit and hope.

Badbeger didn't walk around the table so much as hunt and prowl. He inspected the cluster of balls from all sides, looking for an angle that didn't exist. "You're stripes," Lester reminded him. "But you have to hit the white one first."

"Be quiet," Badbeger said. "I've played this game before."

"I know. You played my photographer friend yesterday. Who won?"

"I did," Badbeger grinned.

"That's not what I heard."

"Aw-haw," the Frenchman snorted. His arrogance was not productive. He miscued, giving Lester a huge advantage.

"Ball-in-hand?"

"No, play it from there."

"Two shots?"

"One shot."

"Now come on, there has to be a penalty for a foul. It's either ball-in-hand or two shots. What are you giving me?"

"Ball-in-hand."

Lester played the same sneaky game that had served him well in the pubs of South London, rolling the balls up to the pockets like Rolls Royces approaching country houses. On all except the easy shots, he returned the white to safety, keeping Badbeger trapped at the baulk end or facing some obtuse double or cut, enjoying watching him twist and squirm around the cue grimacing, making awkward stabbing motions down at the contact ball jammed against the cushion, then watching it squirm off to the side or crash into his colours with no strategy or direction. He sunk a couple of flukes to keep himself in the frame.

It was on the billiard table, Lester mused, that a man's true character emerged. With only one ball left to Badbeger's four, he found himself in the unusual position of being ahead. Would he be able to keep his composure and make his superior intelligence count, or would his competitor find a way to block and crowd him, and eventually overpower him with some random mutation of genetics that meant men like him nearly always got what they desired? Badbeger was in the unusual position of being behind in the game. He was unsure of how or where to play from the edges, as Lester would have been, and was used to. If he was in Julien's position now, Lester would keep making things difficult until an opening appeared, reduce the deficit by one, then retreat. Some might call it boring, or even cheating, to play snookers, but Lester didn't care as long as he triumphed. Sometimes there's nothing more beautiful than winning ugly, or watching somebody ugly win.

Another missed cut into the middle pocket opened up Lester's red on the bottom cushion. He sliced it beautifully, and watched his ball zip with atomic precision along the rail, into the bucket. The black would go straight into the middle. He was pulling his cue back when Badbeger said, "Treble the black."

Lester looked up over the frames of the orange aviators he'd put on for the occasion. "What?"

"That's the Paris rule. The black must hit two cushions before it goes in, and you must do it left-handed with your eyes closed."

"That's preposterous."

"Those are the rules we play."

"I've heard of naming a pocket, even doubling the black. But trebling left-handed with your eyes closed? You're taking the piss."

Lester potted the black right-handed and rolled the cue across the table.

"Oops, I win," Badbeger said.

"Whatever."

"If you don't want to play my rules, then the bet is off." Badbeger shrugged.

So Lester knew how he and his type did it. Reduce the game to one of primordial chance, where the man with the heaviest cue, or the correct star sign, tends to win. "I'm afraid we had an agreement, Julien. Don't make this difficult. I'm on a tight deadline, and don't have time for bullshit."

"Time for what?" Badbeger wasn't so smooth now. "Say that again?"

"I'm busy, I don't have time for..."

"What did you say? I'm being difficult? Are you accusing me?"

"I'm not accusing, I'm saying..."

Badbeger was pure attitude. He was behaviour. He had hands like rocks and a neck like a tree trunk. He squared up to Lester, drew his arm back.

"Don't..." Lester flinched, "hit a man with glasses."

"Are they spectacles?"

"No, they're light-enhancers."

"What's the rule about hitting a man with light-enhancers?"

"You have to do it with your left hand, with your eyes closed."

XXX

Lester convinced Julien Badbeger that he wasn't interested in his arrest for false imprisonment, having allegedly locked a showgirl from the Moulin Rouge in his basement until she read his latest collection of essays. They went to a Chinese restaurant on Rue de Belleville and ordered a huge bowl of pork and cabbage dumplings with noodles in broth, which Lester prodded at, the amphetamines keeping his appetite tied in a ventral knot.

Even while slurping, Badbeger had a magnetism. In addition to his novels, in the last couple of years he'd become a household name as the host of a late-night TV show. *Paris Culture* was a heady mix of book reviews, celebrity gossip, wine tasting, salmon tickling and beef butchery. But it—and he—had remained notably silent on the whereabouts of its most frequent guest.

Lester backwashed his bottle of Tsing Tsao and shaded his eyes from the sun reflecting off the cars outside. "Most of Paris seems content for him to stay lost."

Badbeger looked around again to see if anybody had spotted him. "Paris is not really his audience anymore. He is the intellectual for provincial farmers, patisserie owners and primary school teachers."

"What do they see in him?"

"They know what they are getting with Gérard, like at Monoprix or Carrefour. The quality is not exceptional, but it is everywhere. Or at least, it was."

The wooden benches were starting to cram with students and Chinese. They might be overheard, but it seemed unlikely any spook would venture close enough to end up with a steaming bowl of noodle broth over his head.

Badbegder confirmed that he had been one of Gérard's sinecures, along with Dutronc and a few other trusted friends. He showed Lester his ESCHATON card that gave access to the Bureau of Surrealist Research. It looked official, like a driving licence or identity card, with iridescent strips and hologrammic aspects.

"Ooh, very nice. I met Janice yesterday. She didn't show me hers."

Badbeger dabbed his beard with a napkin. He looked puzzled. "Sorry, who?"

Something inside Lester jolted, like the chain had come off and reality was once again refusing to click into place. "Janice Remarque? Blonde woman, senior executive, twenty years' service. You must know her."

"Maybe I know who you're talking about. Is this the woman who set up the website?"

Lester flicked sweat off his forehead and onto the next table's kimchi. "Yes. We had a productive chat yesterday. She didn't break her NDA or anything, but she said some pretty interesting things, and I'd like to hear what you think."

Badbeger's breath was audible from his massive hairy chest. He was trying to stay calm, but he foresaw trouble. "I have to warn you," he was choosing his words carefully, "that woman is..."

Before he could finish his sentence, Lester sighed. "A pathological liar?"

"Yes. She ought to be locked up, have her tongue cut out."

"What has she said?"

"What hasn't she said?" He spoke with the indignation of a man who had been tormented, accused. "I cannot say too much, because I have also signed an NDA, and believe me, Gérard knows how to enforce them. I would be very interested to know, what did this fantasist tell you?"

"Nothing specific, just that, you know, Gérard was known to react to criticism."

"Is this your notebook?" Badbeger grabbed it and began flipping through the pages.

"Hey, that's confidential, give it back."

Badbeger held it at arm's length and shoved another hand to the reporter's forehead to keep him at arm's length. " 'Janice Remarque, La Cave du Vin, 4pm...' "

Lester ducked under the table and grabbed Badbeger by the balls. "No, just no. There's a line, mate, and you've crossed it."

Badbeger squealed like a little girl, dropped the notebook on the table.

"Alright, as you please. There's nothing in here anyway." A couple of pages had come loose. "Were you recording it, at least?"

"No. Was Gérard?"

"I wouldn't know."

"She told me she worked for him for twenty years. Is that not true?"

"For a short while, back in the early days, she was involved somehow. Before I knew him."

"What happened?"

"She's crazy, mentally unwell, dangerous."

"Was she mad from the beginning, or did the job drive her insane?"

"She's barred from the Surrealist Central, not allowed to come within a hundred metres of Gérard or any of his properties. That's all I know."

"Why?"

"The things she said, the things she published."

"Such as?"

"They were destroyed."

"You mentioned a website. Do you have the address, so I can check it out?"

"No, it's ancient history, we've moved on."

"She told me she co-directed the film, *Gérard & Jacques*."

"I've never heard such nonsense."

"She knew the production in great detail."

"Did she show you a copy of the DVD?"

"No."

"Have you looked it up on IMDB?"

"No."

"I suggest you do."

"But she did show me a pair of the night-vision goggles."

"She stole them from Jacques at the premiere. Sneaked in dressed as a Muslim."

Lester felt a mixture of sadness, relief and frustration. The lithium he'd found in the bathroom cabinet ought to have been a giveaway, but then, Badbeger seemed to be spinning some kind of party line also.

"You wouldn't happen to have any evidence, just to put my mind at rest?"

"They might follow us, but I don't keep tabs on stalkers. Why don't you email ESCHATON or the police? They might be able to send you something."

"I guess I will have to."

Badbeger tossed a fifty on the plate, slung his corduroy jacket over his shoulder as he walked away.

The temperature had dropped to the high twenties since they left the restaurant and were walking down the rickety hill, past the Chinese restaurants and slanted signage of Aux Folies, where Lester's tribe were displaying themselves in vintage clothes and sunglasses, drinking cheap pints.

"Do you plan to get out of Paris for the summer, Julien?"

"Of course, I would not dream of being here for July or August. Nobody who has made anything of themselves stays in Paris then."

"I read in his column, you used to go swimming together?"

"Our weekly ritual. He dictated his columns while he swam."

"I don't suppose there's any chance I could meet him? I can acquire some Speedo's, if those are the rules."

Badbeger smiled like he would to an autograph hunter or a writer pressing a manuscript onto him. "He never swims in public pools. But why don't you give me your card? I'll let you know." Lester had heard that one plenty of times. Still, he scribbled his email and phone number on a page from his notebook and ripped it out. Badbeger tucked it in his shirt pocket and looked over Lester's shoulder for a cab. There were none coming down Rue de Belleville, so Lester still had a few more moments with the sinecure while he hailed one on his phone.

"Do you always play women at billiards?"

"Today was not an exception."

"I mean, do you always make them play for something?"

"They play me for something."

"I suppose. Is it true that you've slept with over a thousand women?"

"Give or take a couple of hundred."

"Has it ever caused you problems?"

"The only problems are the ones who want something more, like children or marriage."

"What about Gérard, has he ever had problems with women extorting money from him, issuing threats, making accusations?"

Badbeger wasn't looking up from his phone. His responses had become terse, and his twitch returned. "My cab is just around the corner."

Lester followed him towards the black BMW parked on Rue Denoyez. Pacing swiftly now to get away from the reporter... the driver wound the window down. "Julien, oui." Badbeger threw himself onto the back seat and slammed the door shut.

"Driver, go!"

"I can't, monsieur, there is a car in front."

Lester opened the door. "One more thing."

"What is it?" Badbeger leaned towards him, as if beckoning him to whisper, then hurled a fist like a medicine ball into his chest. He followed with a left hook to the side of the head that didn't quite connect, but put Lester down.

"Thanks for lending me your photographer. A dark little demon!"

Heaving and wincing, asphyxiating on fumes, Lester lay clutching at his stomach in the gutter as the car rolled down the hill towards the sunset.

XXXI

Janice's phone went straight to voicemail. Still short of breath, Lester texted her asking if they could meet as soon as possible. Kicking through the rotten vegetables on Rue Saint-Denis, he was scrolling through the Internet Movie Database on his phone, about to message Tom Perkins to ask for another favour, when Perkins texted him, telling him to check the front page of the *Daily Hack* immediately.

He went into Chez Jeanette and bought himself a pint of wheat beer to prepare himself. At worst, he thought they might have found Gérard and his story was dead. When he opened the webpage, the news hit him harder than Badbeger's fist.

Before he had time to even take a breath, he was dragged through the portal of his screen and into hell. At first he felt anger, next came the shame, and then the fear. He couldn't even read the whole article or look at the pictures.

An exotic storm brewed inside him. His guts fizzled and squelched. He ran to the bathroom to clean himself up, then came outside to discover that the world was not only indifferent, but sickeningly spiteful towards him. Paris seemed to be bearing down upon him, cooking him alive.

He stared ahead for several minutes, his thoughts screaming at him, and he knew he had to talk to somebody to let those voices out.

"Hello, Tom Perkins, Western Rural News."

His voice cracked. "Can you find out where Wilhelm Gnobb is staying in Paris?"

"Les, Les, calm down."

"Calm down?!"

"Don't do anything silly you might regret. This isn't the end of the world."

Lester screamed, marching up the street then back again, nowhere to vent. " 'Assault?!' They're saying I *assaulted* her?! I'm the one who's been assaulted!"

"Wait, you're saying she assaulted you?"

"No, just now! One of Gérard's henchmen, a novelist called Julien Badbeger punched me."

"Why would he do that?"

"I was doing my job, asking the right questions." Lester snapped a photo of his face, swollen and bruised on the cheek, and sent it to Perkins.

"Les, have you been drinking?"

"Yes, but so what?! People who've had a drink can still get assaulted, can't they? It doesn't make it right!"

"No, no, of course, you're right." Perkins spoke quietly so his workmates couldn't hear. His voice was compassionate, but he seemed sceptical. "Are you alright?"

"No, I don't think I am alright."

"Can you talk now, though? We need to do some crisis management."

"I can talk."

"Alright, talk me through what happened."

Lester paced up and down the Rue Saint-Denis, recounting his hazy memories of Monday night, how he'd gone into the bathroom with Ridicula to do lines.

"I'll stop you there," Perkins said. "Which bathroom did you go into?"

"The women's bathroom. Does it matter? Does that make it worse?"

"Not necessarily. She isn't saying you forced your way in. You went there together, she invited you?"

"Correct. She pretty much *dragged* me in."

"Right, that's one thing. Although, the fact you took a picture in a women's bathroom might be a separate issue. There's a reasonable expectation of privacy. But we can discuss that later. The next obvious problem is the groping and the forced kissing. Did you really slam her against a wall?"

"Look, that's not how it was, okay? You know what it's like when you do some coke with somebody..."

"Actually, I wouldn't."

"It's an intimate experience. Sexually charged. She was rubbing herself up against me. When she asked me to stop, I stopped. That's it, a simple miscommunication. I don't know how she can call this assault. Really, can she?"

"Well, she has, so let's deal with what they have said before we get into how you respond, if you choose to respond."

"Okay."

"Next, there's the issue of the photo, and your attempt at selling it to a tabloid news website."

"This is probably the most disingenuous part. I *did* sell it to a tabloid news website! I sold it to the *Daily Hack*! To Wilhelm Gnobb! He bought it off me for five hundred euros, just like he's bought stuff like this off me before!"

"Really?" Even Perkins seemed surprised by this omission. "Have you got any evidence—emails, bank transfers? This could really help your case."

Lester tried to stop his mind spinning, regain control. "Wait, I don't think there is. Fuck, fuck, fuck."

"Have you checked your outbox?"

"I sent it via encrypted message. They automatically delete."

"Shit. And what about the payment, surely that's traceable?"

"No, he sent it in Bitcoin."

"Oh Les, what are you doing with Bitcoin?"

"Buying drugs off the dark web." He didn't need telling how stupid he was. "Wait, there will be a record that I spoke to Gnobb on the phone, on Monday night. No, it was Tuesday morning by that point."

"Were you recording it?"

"No."

"Contemporaneous shorthand notes?"

"No."

"Alright, so assuming their timeline isn't out, the next morning, Tuesday, you continued harassing her?"

"Harassment? That really is so fucking ludicrous."

"Go on, what happened?"

"My friend called her pretending to be Gérard. He's an impressionist. We were trying to blag a location. That's not illegal, is it?"

"I don't know about French law, but in the UK, subterfuge is certainly frowned upon."

"Frowned upon is fine. At this point I feel like everything I do is *frowned upon*."

"Let's stay focused. Did you beg her to come over and see you, and were you talking about your penis?"

"No, well kind of. Freddy pretended he was Gérard locked in a barn, and he'd got his penis stuck in some machinery. He begged her to help. There was nothing sexual about it."

"I have to ask, do you have a recording of the call?"

"No."

"Contemporaneous shorthand notes?"

"No."

"Presumably you weren't sober at this point?"

"No, we'd been up all night drinking and doing blow."

Perkins sighed and whistled. "Thanks, Les. Can you give me a couple of hours to digest all this, and I'll see what might be the best thing for you to do?"

"Sure."

"In the meantime, you're a member of the union, aren't you?"

"Yup."

"Give your NUJ chapel call. That's what they're there for."

"Good idea, Tom. I'm going to call the goddam union, and we are going to strike back ten times harder than we were hit."

"That's the spirit. Stay off the drink and drugs—if you can."

XXXII

Back in London, the National Union of Journalists' London freelance chapel was about to close for the day. Dave Carney, a former tabloid paparazzi from East Ham with a monotonous, nasal voice, was desperate to get out of the office and catch a couple of hours of sunshine, when an obscure freelance reporter for a magazine he'd never heard of called from Paris. The line was bad and the young man sounded *tired and emotional*, to use the old *Private Eye* euphemism.

"Hold on a moment, son, slow down. I can't hear you very well."

"Try listening, please. I've got a terrible headache. If I don't get a satisfactory response, I'm going to..."

"Son, I advise you not to make threatening remarks to a member of Her Majesty's press."

"Her Majesty's press? Who the fuck do you work for? I pay my subs. I demand legal advice. Put me through to the lawyers."

"I'm sorry, son, all our lawyers are currently having their faces painted by a children's TV presenter at our annual summer party. Ordinarily, I'd be there myself, but I drew the short straw this year."

"Well in that case, what should I do, go over to his hotel and chop his head off?"

"I'm not a lawyer, but I can say with a great deal of certainty that beheading people is illegal in France unless they happen to be monarchs, and even then we caution against it."

"Dave, this is not good enough."

"This is the best we can offer, I'm afraid, son."

"You're making me want to kill myself."

"The NUJ counsels members against suicide. Would you like me to sign you up for our suicide-prevention group-therapy seminar in October?"

"Sign me up. In the meantime, I am not requesting, I am *demanding* representation."

"Okay," Dave sighed, extremely reluctant. "Why don't you give me a brief summary? I'll take some notes and open a new case to add to the backlog."

Lester told his NUJ rep how to access the internet on his computer, then directed him to the front page of the *Daily Hack*.

"Ooh, that is very nasty. Good artwork, though. They've got the mugshot, which I always like to see in a crime story."

"*Crime* story?!"

"They've got you looking like a proper English yob. Oh dear. Oh dear, oh dear. That one at the bar, with the eyes half open, pissed as a newt. That looks like professional papping to me. I wonder if the *Sun* or the *Mail* are interested in this."

"The *Sun* and the *Mail*?! Dave, you're supposed to be representing me, not ruining my career."

"Son, I am merely informing you, I know news editors. I wouldn't be surprised if they pick this up. And until our lawyers are back in the office, there's not a lot I can do for you."

"What do you mean, not a lot you can do? You could put an announcement out demanding a picket of Barkbite News and the *Daily Hack*, for a start. Call Steve Renault, telling him he's on the hook for a huge libel payout if they don't retract and apologise immediately. Get on the phone to *Down N Out!*, telling them your members are boycotting the publication until they honour their agreements. Come on, I want to see some solidarity."

"I'm sorry, son, you're freelance. We don't do solidarity. I've noted your case. I recommend you hold tight until you hear back from head office. Until then, I wish you the very best of..."

"Prick!" Lester screamed and kicked a lamp post.

XXXIII

Lester paced Boulevard Magenta, knocking back Desperado's, when he received a text message from the General Secretary of the Labour Party of Great Britain. Well, well, well, it turned out somebody had been watching him from on high.

"Dear Mr Langway," it read. "It is with regret that you have been suspended from Labour until further notice while we investigate claims of antisemitism against you. Should you wish to appeal, you have ten working days to lodge…"

He had forgotten that he was even a member of Labour party. But still, antisemitism? Had he really stooped that low? The accusations were piling up around him so quickly, he felt so besieged, he could no longer say for sure what was true and what was not. He saw the boulevard ahead of him roll up like a carpet and a waste disposal unit dump him in the Seine.

On the steps of the Saint-Vincent de Paul church, he smoked and drank with the helpless determination of the well and truly ruined. When the verger arrived to lock up for the day, he staggered onwards towards Gare du Nord, swaying, banging into people, crying. He crouched down and considered his prospects. He would most likely be homeless, a true down-and-out in a piss-soaked alley, where the unloved deposited themselves next to the exit portal, as if to say, *don't worry, beautiful people, I'll be out of your reality soon*. He wondered how many of the street hustlers hanging around the elevated train at Barbès had the bug, and considered giving himself to them. Maybe humanity is the disease, he mused, and the "virus" is really the cure for people like me.

He rolled a joint and sat on a park bench on Boulevard Clichy opposite the public lavatories, punishing himself with the stench. He imagined himself six feet under, and what a comparatively peaceful place the ground must be.

With another bump of speed tucked into his glands, he moved through Pigalle's neon sexodromes. His morbid vision was fixed on the window displays of dildos shaped like Eiffel Towers. He imagined ramming them down the throats of the useless and dishonest, battering them over the head, anally raping them, urinating on them, making a bonfire of their corpses, and justifying himself in front of the judge: they *made* me do it, your honour.

At Place Blanche, he darted across the street to avoid the human trash piled up outside the Moulin Rouge and counted the numbers until he reached 42 Rue Fontaine. The old Haussmann terrace had been knocked down and replaced with the Théâtre de la Comedie. On its wall there was a plaque celebrating the life of its previous inhabitant, the leader of the Surrealists, André Breton.

Through tears in his eyes, Lester saw Breton in 1929, pacing the floor of his studio surrounded by primitive masks, sipping an aperitif, summoning vituperation for the *Second Manifesto*, where he would purge the bastards in the group. With the stroke of a pen, Breton would cull them like sheep, sweep them away into the gutters of irrelevance.

André Breton fought at the gates of culture and did not retreat! Lester made a nondenominational gesture of prayer outside his former residence, and the Pope of Surrealism's giant head and backswept hair appeared. They smiled at one another. After a few minutes of quiet contemplation, Lester plugged his headphones in and hauled himself up Rue de Clignancourt. Whether he knew it or not, he was about to start a long, uphill climb. This was the next chapter of his life.

> *Black trombone*
> *Monotone*
> *C'est jolie...*

THURSDAY

XXXIV

All a woman had to do now would be to say that she didn't hate him and Lester would swoon in her arms. He rang the bell and waited. A girl with a jagged bob haircut came downstairs wearing a boyish tshirt and bloojean skirt. When she saw him standing there with a six-pack of Desperado's, Anaïs's eyes lit up like an ice cream parlour in the snow. "What are you doing here?!"

"I hope you don't mind, I'm a bit drunk."

"I don't mind as long as you share with me."

Her apartment on the Chateau Rouge side of Montmartre hill was on the ninth floor without a lift, the former servants' quarters at the top of a spiral staircase with a WC on the outside. She didn't apologise for the mess, nor look embarrassed by the size of the place, half of which was taken up by an old iron bathtub. Men's suits made of old tweed and wool were hung on a three-metre wire that sagged from one side of the human storage box to the other, and on the walls she had pegged three fedora hats to sell at the Clignancourt flea market on Sunday.

Lester ruffled her thick mop that had been chopped onto her head roughly, as if by a florist with big scissors. While he had never really taken much notice of fashion, he now understood the significance of a woman changing her hair.

"You like it?"

"I love it. You're a proper *gamine* now."

"You told me how much you love that film, so I went and got the poster."

He'd been too busy admiring her transformation into an androgynous urchin to notice that above her bed, she'd put up a poster for Louise Malle's 1960 adaptation of *Zazie dans le Métro*. Ah! Her resemblance to the mischievous main character was striking.

Lester and Anaïs cracked open a couple of beers. He rolled them a joint and put on Françoise Hardy's 'Tous les garçons et les filles', a song about the sadness of outsiders who want to know what love feels like. Nodding their heads from side to side, Anaïs slid her fingers across the tracking pad of a laptop balanced on a stool, adjusting the contrast on one of her poster designs, trying not to pay too much attention to the dishevelled mess of a man who was sitting very close to her, eyeing up the tops of her soft, milky thighs that were visible below the short bloojean skirt.

"What do you think? Tell me if it's shit."

"I like it a lot," he said. "After my name, get rid of '*Down N Out!*' and put, 'independent researcher.'"

"Cool," she said, without asking questions, still smiling at the music and how it suited the situation. "How many of them are you going to print?"

"As many as I can with a hundred euros."

"You can probably make fifty."

"Great."

"Where do you want to put them up?"

"Outside lawyers' offices around Saint-Germain. If we have any left, art galleries and bookshops. I want them to be seen by anyone who might have dirt on Gérard."

"Don't forget the Surrealist Central."

"How could I forget? That's a great idea. Would you like some speed?"

"Mmm, I love speed!"

Anaïs drank and took her drugs like a boy, and he liked that. He lay back on the bed with his can of Desperado's, closed his eyes and saw himself as Jean-Paul Belmondo in those early New Wave films by Godard and Melville. When he opened his eyes, Anaïs was looming over him, inspecting the bruise on the side of his face. "Who did this to you?"

"I did it to myself."

"Lester, don't beat yourself up."

They kissed.

XXXV

Lester was at one end of the bath and Anaïs was at the other. It wasn't a very big bath, more like a big rusty bucket. Their knees were sticking out and the water was turbid. The stereo played a sultry downbeat jazz song, 'Le Cinéma' by Claude Nougaro. When Lester appeared to be drifting off to sleep, Anaïs flicked her big toe against the water and giggled when it splashed him in the face. He looked up and noticed that she was doodling in a black book.

"Are you drawing me?"

"I'm wondering who you are."

"Please don't."

"I write psychoanalytic profiles of the people I care about most."

"What are your observations so far?"

"I'm only getting started. I need more information. Do you think you're insane?"

"No, I'm the sanest man alive."

"What does it mean to be sane in an insane society?"

He hadn't thought of it like that. Maybe that's why he needed the antidepressants. Anaïs grabbed a book from next to the record player, *The Divided Self* by RD Laing. "Have you ever read this?"

"No, what's it about?"

"There is the story of the patient in a lie detector who was asked if he was Napoleon," she read. "He replied, 'No'. The lie detector recorded that he was lying. Anyway, each of us has his own autonomous sense of identity and his own definition of who and what he is. You are expected to be able to recognise me. That is, I am accustomed to expect that the person you take me to be, and the identity that I reckon myself to have, will coincide. However, if there are discrepancies of a sufficiently radical kind remaining after attempts to align them have failed, there is no alternative that one of us must be insane."

"Do you think you're insane?"

"Yes."

"I disagree, but continue."

"I have no difficulty in regarding another person as psychotic if, for instance, he says he is Napoleon, whereas I say he is not. *Or if* he says I am Napoleon, whereas I say I am not."

"Or if he says he is Lester Langway, journalist, and they say he is just a bum."

"*Or if* he thinks that I wish to seduce him, whereas I think that I have given him no grounds in actuality for supposing that such is my intention."

The bathwater was getting cold and a cool breeze intruded through the window. Lester grabbed a towel. "I'm getting chilly, aren't you?"

As he lay on the bed, thunder cracked outside. Chaos had sparked in the tendrils of the city. The Eiffel Tower underwent electroconvulsive therapy. Rain streamed down the windows like the credits to a film in reverse. When Anaïs stepped out of the bath, she did so with the wobbly grace of a prematurely aged grandmother. She climbed on top of him, and he rubbed his hands along her pale, nacreous thighs. With her Cheshire cat grin widening and her body lowering onto his, he knew that he would remember this image, and this feeling, for the rest of his life.

XXXVI

Anaïs didn't wake up like most people. She wriggled out of her dreams. She kept a dream diary, but not a regular diary. This was her mode of existence, her mode of being, dreams. Although most of her dreams were so haunting, they might be construed as nightmares.

When she wriggled out of her latest nightmare, Lester had changed into one of her tweed suits and fedora hats, and was making coffee on the stove. "Look at you, Mr Detective," she said as he gave her the cup.

He perched on the edge of the bed and showed her the books he'd taken from the shelf and would be borrowing: *Psychomagic* by Alejandro Jodorowsky and *The Theatre, Its Double* by Antonin Artaud.

"My friend gave me the Jodorowsky as a present. Look inside, it's inscribed to me. I still haven't read it."

He ruffled her hair. "In that case, I'll make sure I look after it."

They reaffirmed their feelings with touch, assuring each other that they would no longer have to suffer alone, that they were now a team. Anaïs wanted Lester to come back to bed, and he wished he could. But for his own peace of mind, he had to carry on as though nothing had happened and hope that the rest of the world would forgive him now that he had a reason to be a better man.

"But won't you let me tell you about my dream?"

"Go on, then."

"I dreamed that I took you back to Brittany to meet my father."

"This sounds ominous."

"Have I told you about my father?"

"Bits and pieces. You're not in contact anymore?"

"Occasionally he sends me presents. But in this dream, you sent him a present. It was a chocolate inside a Christmas card. But when he ate it, it poisoned him."

"I'm sorry about that."

"No, you did a good thing! I can't wait for my father to die so I inherit his little house, all his books and records, and then I won't have to work anymore."

"Are you going to work today?"

"No, I got fired."

"How are you feeling?"

"I don't know. Do you think what we did was a sin?"

"Poisoning your father?"

"No, last night."

"Why do you ask?"

"Because my father sent me to a school run by nuns. They brainwashed me with their propaganda since I was a child."

"That's all it is, propaganda."

"Okay." She didn't seem entirely convinced, like when you tell a child the earth is round. "Where are you going?"

"I have a couple of meetings, but I should be done by evening. Can you make the wheat paste and get started with the posters?"

"Sure."

He left her a list of locations and a hundred-euro note. Thinking about her situation then, he turned back and kissed her on the head, peeled off another ten. "Treat yourself to a big breakfast."

XXXVII

Last night's storm really cleared the air. When Lester walked down the Rue Clignancourt in his suit and hat, smoking a cigarette, he not only looked but felt like a different man. For the first time since he arrived in Paris, he was comfortable in his own skin, and his shoes were soft and spongey, like walking across a lush spring lawn.

He chewed a couple of magic mushrooms to enhance the experience and started to feel light-headed when he hit the Rue du Faubourg Montmartre, with the colours of the fruit and vegetables bouncing around his retinas, the window displays fizzing and popping with extracts of visual perfume, and the perspective of the gauntlet stretched out as if he was walking through a living, evolving tusk constructed out of civilization's bones.

Under the curly red sign for Le Bouillon Chartier, waiters in pristine white uniforms were opening the doors to the legendary bistro. Crossing Boulevard Haussmann, he followed the slope that forked to the left, onto Rue Montmartre, looking for his location. Passing it a couple of times and circling back to the side corner entrance, a fire exit was propped open to reveal a red-carpeted stairwell. He got up one flight and came upon the club reception desk where he was greeted by a rake-thin woman with ermine features, fussing over a guest book. "Hello, monsieur, can I scan your membership card?"

He peered through a hexagram and into a lounge area with low red lights. "I'm not a member, but I'm interested in joining. Would it be possible to take a tour?"

"Of course. I'll sign you in." She pushed a leather guest book across to him. He flipped back a few pages and didn't see much action.

Her hand swooped in, turned the pages pack, finger pointing. "Just here, sir. Next to today's date. Name and signature."

Swoosh.

"If you'd like to come this way, Monsieur Britton."

The receptionist led him through an empty, dimly lit room on many levels with indoor greenery and black leather sofas set around low tables. The speaker system played hip-hop beats laced with sitar. On the walls, sepia photos of a stern-looking termagant in a Russian peasant hat, the poet William Butler Yeats, some western colonialist gentlemen, as well as eastern prayer symbols, numerological charts, old maps of India and the town of Adyar.

"That's Helena Blavatsky," the receptionist said, pointing to the portrait. "Our spiritual mother."

Grasshoppers hatched in his tummy, a giddy sensation. Colours swirled in patterns. The plant in the corner turned into an iguana bearing its teeth at him.

At the bar there was a young Indian fellow dressed in black with long hair like a rock star, sipping an espresso and making notes on his digital device. "I'll pass you over to Sanjay, our leader."

"Hello, Mr..."

"Britton, Andrew Britton."

Sanjay offered a soft, manicured claw with exceptionally long nails. Lester snapped his hand away, terrified.

"Are you okay, Mr Britton?"

He stared at Sanjay's hand, frightened. "Yes, it's just..."

Sanjay made an effort to remain friendly as Lester pointed at the long nails, aghast. But Sanjay's natural charm couldn't hide the contempt in his voice. "You say you'd like to *join* our club of honoured and respected ladies and gentlemen?"

Lester aimed for a golf-club tone, but his tongue had turned to metal. His thoughts were flying by so quickly, he attempted to trap them with sound claps. But he could only blurt out single words before they zoomed past.

Sanjay suspected the guest was mentally challenged and made a move to usher him out the door to an ambulance or taxi. "I'm sorry, Mr Britton, would you like to..."

"Join!"

Sanjay rubbed his hands together nervously, looking for a way to get this loony out of here, although he hadn't hired security.

"What brings you to Paris?"
"GÉRARD."
At the mention of his name, Sanjay's eyes widened in reverence.
"Gérard? An exceptional, learned man!"
"Derenne."
"Yes, we happen to be admirers of Gérard, and have in fact invited him to come and see our new space for great individuals. We are still awaiting his response. We are, after all, a new branch of the Theosophical Society that I myself founded in 2010. The Hotel Blavatsky is an esoteric club, and we practise Helena Blavatsky's methods of cultural and spiritual enlightenment. What is it you do, Mr Britton? Are you a mathematician, perhaps, some sort of prodigy?"
"Poet."
"A poet! I love poetry, especially William Butler Yeats, a member of the Theosophical Society from 1887. What kind of poetry is it you write?"
"Surreal."
"Of course. If you join Hotel Blavatsky, you won't have to shake hands with anybody you don't want to."
It was weird how much power Gérard's name had. A magical vibration in the air. Lester was determined to use it to full effect and see how many doors opened.
"Gérard and his people are exactly the kind of clientele we welcome into our ranks."
Sanjay opened another heavy door into a slippery blue cave that smelled of chlorine. A star had fallen through the roof and smashed a hole in the floor. The lagoon was empty and still. Dolphins could be heard in the distance.
"Here it is, my pride and joy, the hexagram swimming pool."
An 18-year-old with a big, meaty chest was reclining on a towel in a pair of circular hippy sunglasses, reading a book by Gérard.
"How's it going, Mimi?"
"Is the Colonel Olcott room still available on Friday night for my tarot party?"

"As far as I can recall," Sanjay smiled nervously. Then to Lester, as they moved on with the tour: "That's Mimi Renault. She's a Twanky model. What do you think so far, Mr Britton?"

"Tittyfuck!"

"This way, Mr Britton."

Lester's ears popped as they exited the pool area. His anxiety heightened now he couldn't find his way out. In another long, black corridor, he wondered how long he'd been gone, and was disturbed by the thought that he might have lost his mind permanently. Maybe he had landed in a different realm with no laws about what it was permissible to do with the mentally ill.

His phone vibrated. He panicked, wondered why his body was shaking. "Bathroom?"

"The bathroom is through the doors to your right. Would you like me to accompany you?"

"No."

Lester walked as quickly as he could down the corridor, pulsing with creepy vibes. He locked himself in a cubicle and made sure there was nobody listening. The call rang out. He dug his keys into the bag of speed and rushed one in for clarity. A few deep breaths while leant against the toilet wall, he pulled himself together just enough to handle an electronic system.

"Hello, Tom Perkins, Western Rural News."

"Hotel Blavatsky?"

"Sounds fancy. The sheep were quite a story, since you ask. But I guess I'll wait until we can grab a pint to give you the full story."

"Yes?"

"The reason I'm calling: I did some research into... let me find my notes... the Fabian Society of..."

"Umm."

"No, no the Fabian Society of Umm, the Fabian Society of France."

"Ah."

"Unlike the British version of the Fabians, there's not much information about them. It seems to be small and relatively new, but

I did find out who the founder and current chief executive officer is."

"What?"

"I don't know if the name means anything to you, but it's a fellow called Marc Remarque."

He didn't see any significance in this strange crackling of consonants and vowels.

"Listen, are you off your rocker again?"

"Maybe."

"What have you taken?"

"Mushrooms."

"Are you sure that's a good idea?"

"No."

"What are you doing, Les?"

"Having a meltdown."

"Good luck with that. Call me when you're back on earth."

Lester had an ashen look on his face when he came back out. His pupils were heavily dilated, so he slipped his wing-mirror shades back on. He wondered if he'd been gone minutes or hours.

"Mr Britton, good to see you again. You know, I thought I had seen you before. Were you at the Café de Bore on Monday?"

Gulp. "I have to leave."

"Hold on a moment, Mr Britton. I would like to invite you back upstairs for tea and discuss a way we might work together. As you have seen, what I have created is not just a social club, a bar, nor a nightspot. Primarily, we are a society for individuals seeking enlightenment—especially those who are already enlightened. We are looking to forge new alliances with elite individuals and groups. Access to our club costs 3,000 euros a year, but I would be happy to offer you an honorary membership if you were able to connect us with Gérard, or one of Gérard's people, who have so far been rather difficult to pin down. I have a contact for a woman called Simone Gordon, but her emails..."

Lester ran upstairs and back through the empty club. "Mr Britton, please don't go! Aren't you interested in helping us find the next World Teacher?!"

Outside he breathed a big sigh of relief. He needed a drink to make the paranoid thoughts go away. But with Sanjay running after him down the street, he jumped in a cab and slammed the door.

"Place de Clichy!"

XXXVIII

"Alright, Langway?" The innocuous man with a severe haircut and black combat jacket turned from the bar of the Cyrano.

"Mushroom!" Lester sprang onto him, legs off the ground, wrapped himself around his waist. Of all the people he might see in Paris, he never expected to get a text from his vanguard soldier friend—his mentor from the Falkland Islands and third-year university housemate. One of the freest men, one of the most audacious and disdainful minds Lester had ever known! He owed to him, in large part, his ability to take his distance from literature and its tainted charms. Lester saw in Mushroom largely what he wanted to see, to the point where some might have wondered whether Mushroom's persona wasn't invented by Lester from whole cloth.

"I'm being chased by Theosophists."

"Theosophists, eh?" He looked distrustful of them, as though they might be more dangerous than they let on. Lester and Mushroom took one the few tables in the Belle Époque bolt hole. The decorative gold angel above the bar flapped her wings at Lester. "You know this place?"

"No, but I've heard it mentioned somewhere." The tiled walls became a shifting mosaic whose underlying strangeness illustrated the determining value of fortuitous coincidence.

"The Surrealists held their meetings in the back room."

"Explains a lot."

"What does it explain?"

Fetching the Breton biography from his bag... "There, he circled it!"

"Who circled what?"

"Nevermind. How was it?"

"How was what?"

"Iraq, Afghanistan?"

A lot had happened since Mushroom left their student house to train at the Sandhurt Military Academy. Three years later, he exited the Middle Eastern Theatre of War on a stretcher, honourably discharged with his tibia blown off, replaced with a prosthetic.

"Are you a pacifist now?"

"Hell no! I love my prosthetic. I've convinced Phoebe of its erotic potential. We're married now."

Lester glugged at a pint, adjusted his tie, sweating into the rim of his fedora. "Congratulations! Still killing for Queenie?"

"Nah, I've given it up, mate."

Lester slapped his old drinking buddy's hand, wiggling his fingers—their special handshake.

"I've gone freelance."

"Hitman?"

"War consultant. I give seminars to generals and arms industry people looking for a psychological edge. You make more money talking about wars than fighting in them."

"You should write a novel."

"It's weird you're carrying that Breton book. I teach Surrealism, and the Surrealists were forbidden from writing novels."

"What the fuck?"

"I start every seminar with one of Breton's stories from the First World War. 'There was a young, well-educated man who, in the front lines, had aroused the concern of his superior officers by a recklessness carried to extremes: standing on the parapet in the midst of the bombardments, he conducted the grenades flying by with his finger. His explanation for the doctors was as simple as could be: strange as it may seem, and although this ploy was not new, he had never been wounded. But underneath, some clearly heterodox certainties were being articulated: the supposed war was not only a simulacrum, the make-believe shells could do no harm, the apparent injuries were only makeup... Naturally, the doctors did everything in their power to make this man admit that the outsized costs of such a spectacle could not simply be for his personal benefit, but it seemed to me he didn't really believe it.' Then I say to the generals, let's start from the assumption that the man in that anecdote is right, that the war is happening in our own heads. What then?"

"What then?"

"There's a reading list. The Manifestoes, *The Automatic Message*, *Nadja*, *Paris Peasant*, *Diary of a Genius*. Automatic writing, the paranoid critical method, seances."

"What a coincidence."

"We work with petrifying chance, extraordinary coincidence."

"Are you subverting from the inside?"

"Remember, the Surrealists were soldiers before they were Surrealists. Where did Breton develop his ideas? In a military hospital, reading Freud, and from Jacques Vaché's *War Letters*."

"Ah, yes, I was going to ask you..."

"The idea is to give the generals a superior reality system. I'm teaching them to go literally above realism."

"Know anything about Gérard Derenne?"

"The philosopher?"

"The wanker."

Lester told him about some of the petrifying coincidences that had happened: the Breton book, the Bureau of Surrealist Research, a man pretending to be Jacques Vaché turning up to collect his parcel.

Mushroom nodded his big, square head and moved on.

"Want to try some of the techniques?"

"I'll try anything."

"Let's try a Dada exercise for composing a poem."

"Alright, let's do it."

"Take a newspaper. Take some scissors." Mushroom plucked them from the air. "Choose from this paper an article of the length you want to make your poem. Cut out the article. Next carefully cut out each of the words that makes up this article and put them all in a bag. Shake gently. Next take out each cutting one after the other. Copy conscientiously in the order in which they left the bag. The poem will resemble you. And there you are—an infinitely original author of charming sensibility, even though unappreciated by the vulgar herd."

"I'm done with the cut-up method," Lester said, pushing the scattered clippings away. "The *Columbia Journalism Review* has accused me of plagiarism, amongst other things."

"Totally ridiculous. They should come and see what goes on in Afghanistan. The way the men treat women, that's *assault*. But if you bring that up, they'll accuse you of being Islamophobic."

After the antisemitism claims, he wanted to steer clear of any other kind of racial -phobia. "You're freelance now? Fancy doing a job for me?"

"What kind of job?"

"This prick who wrote the article, Wilhelm Gnobb. I don't suppose it would be possible..."

"I'm going to stop you there, mate. I can't engage with plots or actions against named individuals. I can only talk in general terms about psychological warfare and unexplained deaths. You never know, maybe I'll drop a few hints along the way."

"Drop them bombs."

"So after the Second World War, did you know, with the help of Nazi scientists, the Americans experimented with mind control using psychedelic drugs and psychic programming? The name of the programme was MK-ULTRA."

"Seriously?"

"Let me finish. It's a historical fact that the CIA conducted illegal drug trials. It was revealed in the Rockefeller Commission, although most of the files were destroyed. It's another fact that the CIA used hypnotists and other mystics to brainwash subjects. Military doctors and hypnotists developed techniques to alter a person's consciousness, disorientate them so they didn't know where they were, and created new behavioural patterns, new personalities, new memories. One of the CIA's own men, Frank Olson, threw himself out of a window after a handler spiked his drink with acid. There's plenty of evidence to suggest that Robert Kennedy's assassin, Sirhan Sirhan, had been hypnotised. Observers who witnessed the event said he appeared to be in a trance-like state, and he claimed to have no memories of the incident. There's less compelling evidence that Charles Manson had been programmed at an LA clinic funded by the CIA, that he himself used their brainwashing techniques. Lee

Harvey-Oswald was under the influence of the CIA hypnotist David Ferrie. One of the main players, who crops up throughout the history of CIA brainwashing and occult research is Andrija Puharich, who brought Uri Geller to work for the American government..."

"Hold on," Lester interrupted. "I met Uri Geller at a party on Monday."

"Did he conduct any mind-control on you?"

"Not to my knowledge. Although... wait. Do you really believe this stuff?"

Mushroom stared. "Of course. Want me to demonstrate it?"

"Does it work if I'm already on mushrooms?"

"LSD, DMT or mescaline would be preferable, but there's no reason psilocybin shouldn't have similar effects."

"And what are the effects?"

"They can be numerous. Some people use it to stop smoking or drinking. For others, it's barely noticeable, it just creates an aura of calm. Some parapsychology researchers, such as Dr David Luke at the University of Greenwich, have found test subjects who are capable of reliving past lives or 'remote viewing', seeing things from different times and places as though they're actually there. In a trance state, I know from personal experience that you enhance your natural 'occult' powers of extra-sensory perception. Combined with hallucinatory substances such as psilocybin, you may even have a religious or spiritual experience."

"How long will it last?"

"Only a few hours."

"Go on, then."

XXXIX

Mushroom had Lester close his eyes and slowed down his breathing, checked his pulse. He rapped into his ear, logorrheic verbal outputs. The psilocybin that Lester had administered to himself gave the psy-ops manipulator access to the labile parts of his subconscious. He felt detached from his corporeal existence. His internal monologue cut out. He became a vibration, a protocol.

The waitress shook him awake. "Sir, your friend paid your bill. Would you like another drink?"

"Drink?" Lester looked around for clues to his whereabouts. "What time is it? Where did Mushroom go?"

"Nearly 4.30pm."

An old bohemian at the next table tapped Lester on the shoulder. "That was one of the most interesting conversations I have eavesdropped in a long time."

Lester simpered, unable to speak.

"Your friend asked me to give you this. Return it to the rare books section of Shakespeare and Company."

Lester took the copy of the book, a 1920 first edition of *The Magnetic Fields* by Breton and Soupault, and stuffed it in his bag without saying a word, along with a copy of an "alternative news" magazine the old man slipped to him with a wink, called *Factor X*.

The magazine was zinging with bad design and weird headlines on subjects such as mind control, consciousness manipulation, shamanic mysteries, UFOs, ayahuasca cults, chaos magick, the biosphere, and the creation of the superhuman. Not something he would ordinarily read, but he wasn't feeling like his normal self.

He left the Cyrano and headed towards the centre of Paris as if some rhythm beneath the cobblestones had taken over him. Every sensation was perfect pleasure, absolutely as it should be.

He took his usual route through Square du Temple and Rue des Archives. His cravings for beer and all other earthly delights had been flushed from his system. When he got to the famous bookshop on the Left Bank where he had met Dutronc, the crowds did not affect him. He put on the night-vision goggles he had taken from Janice before he entered the antiquarian section and placed the book on the counter without saying a word. Sitting on the steps opposite, he was a tree that suddenly became aware that its roots went far deeper into the earth than its branches stretched above it—a thousand times deeper.

He reached out with his senses, expecting every moment to be vibrant and tingle. And in turn, the city and his own personality rewarded him with a warm glow, a buzzing on the surface that captured the pulsing essences of matter, and his connection to the stone walls, the linden trees, the filth in the gutters. Instead of the general disorder that pervaded his consciousness and gave him manic anxiety, he condensed every thought into a manageable block, and spread his attention thick, like butter, onto each image, each word, each sound.

He opened a poetry anthology, turned it upside down, and felt like the poet Yeats was speaking directly to him in 'A Vision':

> While on the shop and street I gazed
> My body of a sudden blazed;
> And twenty minutes more or less
> It seemed, so great my happiness
> That I was blessed and could bless.

He took out Anaïs's books then, *Psychomagic* by Jodorowsky and *The Theatre, Its Double* by Artaud, held them up, felt their mass. They did not weigh a thing. He tossed them up in the air and they floated.

A vacuum of air sucked around him, then time reversed. First he saw the blood and limbs detach themselves from the folks in the bookshop. As if in slow motion, he felt their screams penetrate his auditory canals. The windows shattered and sprayed across the street like champagne. The bang, a hundred times louder than thunder, smashed through his ear drums. His brain rattled in his skull like a rubber ball in a tumble dryer. The sky shuddered, Lester felt it falling towards him. He held out his arms to stop white zeppelins from crushing him and saw shreds of paper, torn like confetti, their shadows casting magnified signs onto the cracked carapace of the 6th arrondisement—dazzle! These right-out-of-the-box lightning treatments in Cabaret where, screaming, old psychological knots embellished with the zest of the spectator. Spontaneous human combustion! A wisp of critical sense, skepticism at the breathtaking performance, five hundred people, somebody call an ambulance!—a human head rolled past his feet—and the iron doubt, as these evenings are garnished with complexes and traumas are exposed to broad daylight then with a clever spiritual-analytical "reality show," the real consequences, the poetry that embodies riots, theatre transforms into ritual sacrifice, and in which a real witch, armed with a kitchen knife, where did the madman go?!

The library of Alexandria can be burned down! There are forces above and beyond papyrus! Excessive facilities are no longer available! A culture without space or time, restrained by the capacity of our own nerves, will reappear with all the more energy! Ball lightening! It is right that cataclysms occur which compel us to return to nature! The wick effect! We ended up being so, after observing some dangerous acts perpetrated by hot-tempered individuals, a poltergeist! These experiences shook us up and made us question ourselves seriously. The planet is a giant cremulator! A Japanese haiku provided a key. A student brought the master his poem, which stated:

> A butterfly:
> take away the wings
> and it turns into a pepper!

The old totemism of animals, stones, objects capable of discharging thunderbolts, costumes impregnated with bestial essences—everything, in short, that might determine, disclose, and direct the secret forces of the universe, was a dead thing. The earth trembles every six days! The country's floor itself was, literally, convulsive. Everyone was subject to a tremor—either physical and existential.

Ivan Boris

We do not inhabit a robust world, a bourgeois order supposedly well ingrained, but a trembling reality. Nothing remains fixed, everything trembles, lived precariously, as much in the material plane as in the relational. Guests threw themselves out the window. Naturally, anguish was at the heart of all this craziness.

Lester stole an arm from a cadaver. He hid it in a coat sleeve and amused himself by shaking hands with people, touching them with the dead hand. Most of the time people are content with small innocuous acts, until one day—"crack"—they lose control, they get furious, they break everything, hurl insults, they succumb to violence, sometimes committing a crime... A criminal was familiar with the poetic act, he sublimated his homicidal expression by staging an equivalent act. That's right. Society has put up barriers so that fear and its expression, violence, do not spring up at every moment. Jihad! Carrying out an act is a conscious process that aims at voluntarily introducing a fissure into the dead order that permeates society; it is not the compulsive demonstration of a blind rebel. The second coming of Christ! The screams of an audience, not an actor, the god that sleeps in museums, for theatre as for culture, it remains a question of naming and directing shadows. "Iodine!" The smell of cat urine, victims burnt at the stake, signalling through flames.

Like the plague, the theatre is the time of evil, the triumph of the dark powers that are nourished by a power even more profound than extinction. "A miracle worker!" Revenge of a welfare queen? A slippery world which is committing suicide without noticing it! What is the definition of the poetic act? It can lead to violence. The poetic act is a call to reality: One must face one's own death, the unforeseen, our own shadow, the worms that swarm inside of us. There can be found a nucleus of men capable of imposing their superior notion of the theatre. Poetry is convulsive! It's bound up in the earth's tremors! It denounces appearances; it pierces lies and conventions with its sword. As reality dissolves, one eye in the land of the blind. Destruction is an end in itself! Guilt is useless. A mistake is permitted if it is committed only once and as part of a sincere search for knowledge. "Not again!" This is the human condition:

man seeks knowledge. And what is a man in search of something if not, by definition, an erratic being? Error is an integral part of the journey. We abandon the negative experience, but without any remorse. We have opened the door to the true poetic act! To make the tortilla, you have to break the eggs.

Medics took the audience to the cellar, to the rest rooms, or to the rooftops. The secret history of the USA. The secret space age. Big Brother technology. The end of the Mayan calendar and the countdown to judgment day. They lied to us in Sunday school! Crop circles, lights and orbs. Dirty medicine! Dirty electricity, underwater ruins from prehistoric to modern times, the expanding earth, judgement day!

A large ballet in a cemetery. A strong act, the dance of the living among the dead. The virgin's ascending! One can also make an "ephemeral" act in the ocean, in an airplane, in a very fast train, in a maternity ward, a slaughterhouse, a nursing home, a prehistoric cave, a gay bar, a convent, or at a funeral. Climate change! What is really going on?! Sky critters, the lost book of Enki, the expanding earth! UFOs, exopolitics and disclosure, sacred geometry and unified fields. Gulf War syndrome, myalgic encephalomyelitis, and chronic fatigue syndrome, slaughter of the innocent!

In reality Jesus was a son of King Abgarus of Edessa, a princeling with a small realm, a large treasury, even bigger ambitions. But the wise prince of northern Syria came up against an intractable Rome. Mankind could never have evolved in the available time span from from an ape-like bipedal hominid to homo sapiens with a massive brain. The Jesus and Mary bloodline conspiracy, the landing lights of Magonia, ancient aliens on Mars, exposing the 70-year conspiracy at Roswell to suppress the truth. Myths and meditations, the cosmic window appointment calendar, walking a sacred path, a doctor came and extracted a bit of blood from each one of them. This blood was spilled in a glass that Lester drank. He went off on a long speech about bread, wine, supper, the Last Supper, all the while telling himself that since he had been so crazy as to organise these happenings, he would now have to face the consequences of his own acts. When he finally decided to drink the blood, it had coagulated. As creator of the ephemeral panic, it was impossible to draw back: he therefore had to not drink but eat the blood of his flock. Beyond the outrageous or scandalous character of such experiences, they have value as initiation rites. They force you to go, if only for a moment, beyond attraction and repulsion, beyond cultural conditioning, beyond the criteria of beauty and of faith.

    Lester cut the warped air with scissors and ran through the pierced ether. "A CORPSE?" Big white letters. Strips of architectural paper popped and cracked from the walls like cinders. Gérard's tanned face melted onto the buildings, electro-tanned by the apocalypse microwave. Flakes of burnt kebab meat rotating in the dizzy summer fumes of blaring ciao! ciao! and the white scarf like a rag set alight with petrol. His eyes were demonic like cigarette burns. Inside job! Jujitsu motions would be no help here. Phone signals were jammed. A woman in a baby-doll dress screaming imitations of bombs dropping, the fire of Dresden contained within her, flies buzzing around her head like a cow. Geoffrey Boycott appears on the scene in cricket whites splattered in blood, the corridor of uncertainty! News reports and policemen coinciding into babble. Meat wagons with giant trumpets mounted on them broadcast therapeutic mantras. The Champs-Élysées has been set on fire! The cops piled in from vans, human battlements formed, the smoke rose and the sound of coughing as Lester tried again to find himself as he pushed through a door. She could not have already been inside, could she? "Move along! Move along!" Shields and guns, scraping him towards another bomb. "I'm looking for my friend, please monsieur can you help?" She can't be far away, her propaganda was localised, it was plastered all over the Saint-Germain disaster zone. Gérard's hair flecked with real bone, straggles of singed hair, swabs of crackling flesh. "Anaïs?! Anaïs?!" Nino Ferrer croons *Looking for you*... There were no checkpoints, only shelters and ruins.

FRIDAY

XL

There was no denying it, Mike Conway looked demonic. His flesh was ghostly white, he had a manicured pointy beard and ears shaped like Aces of Spades. He ushered Lester and Anaïs from the Cadet Métro in tight black jeans and a pair of Satan sandals. "I hope the white nationalists, or whoever, haven't got it in for all the independent bookstores," he smiled. Mike entered the door code and led them through the courtyard of 11 Rue de la Chaussée-d'Antin. "Edmond Bailly opened Librairie de L'Art Independent here in 1887. It was, and continues to be, a hermetic enclave. We're not officially open to the public. I operate a selective entrance policy. How did you find me?"

"Some old conspiracy magazine? I don't remember the name." Lester rummaged around in his pockets, but couldn't find it. Anaïs's two books and the magazine he'd been given at the Cyrano had been blown to smithereens. All he had left was a shred of paper that he pulled from his suit pocket: a classified ad for Mike Conway's Syncretic School of Occult Therapies.

"That must be ten years old at least. Where were you during the blast?"

The library was chilly. Lester clutched Anaïs. She was pale and goosebumps had appeared on her skin. "We were outside."

"Sorry to hear that. I never set foot in that bookshop as a matter of principle. The news says the bomber was some white working-class kid they wouldn't let sleep there."

Lester rubbed the back of his neck, pangs of something resembling a memory making him uncomfortable. "They got him in custody?"

"No, they reckon he's dead. What were you doing there?"

"The last four hours are a mystery to me. I remember almost nothing after 4pm."

"You must be suffering post-traumatic amnesia. Would you like some absinthe?"

"I would love some. Anaïs?" They grabbed the green potion with shaking hands. "How did you get into magic, Mike?"

"I was thirteen when I saw Aleister Crowley on the *Sgt. Pepper* album cover. I wondered, who is that? So I went to the library and quickly became a Thelemite, joined the Swindon branch of the Church of Satan. I was its only member."

The basement was crammed with esoteric matter. Enclaves of books and journals. Lester sneezed, popped an allergy pill from his wallet. On the wall above a large upholstered chair with a reading light was André Breton's dismembered head in a print of Clovis Trouille's *The Sleepwalking Mummy*.

"I get a lot of enquiries from collectors and independent researchers such as yourself. Normally they want to see my original Symbolist engravings, obscure occult reviews. Most of the artifacts have a special resonance because they were either written, edited or published in Bailly's original bookshop at this address. Like my original Debussy sheet music, or the *Wagnerian Review*. Although most of the material here isn't for sale. The title of this painting by Rops is *The Devil's Virtue is in His Loins*—a subversive nod to St Augustine, I believe..."

In the image, a callipygian female skeleton clutched the severed head of John the Baptist. Mike lit gas lamps and brought the needle down on an old gramophone. Erik Satie's *Gnossienne #1* twinkled, haunting. Lester wanted to stay and hide, bury himself in antiquity, which seemed safer than the modern world upstairs.

"Wait, I recognise this one." *The Secret Doctrine* by Madame Blavatsky, first edition. Lester sneezed. "I was at her lodge yesterday."

"Yes, some hipsters named a nightclub named after her. If you want to understand what's happening today, you're scratching around the right place. Not the nightclub, the society. Theosophists were in the foreground of occult Paris in the 1880s, and that's where this uprising springs from."

"How so?"

"For example, Gerald Encausse was in the Theosophical Society. He founded the Martinists under the name 'Papus' in this shop.

During a séance, Papus's protégé René Guénon received instruction from the last leader of the Knights Templar—the group that would become the Freemasons—blessing him to reform the secret elite order. At the end of the 19th Century, Guénon and other esoteric groups who met here proposed a radical alternative to anarchy: synarchy, total government ruled by an occult order of great men. Or as Julius Evola called them, absolute individuals who embodied the supremacy of the will. The SS were essentially an occult guard based at Wewelsburg castle."

"Hold on, let me write this down." Claude Debussy's *Arabesque* suite now twinkled from the bronze horn. "What's that got to do with the bombing of a bookshop?"

"The news says the kid who bombed the shop may have been a member of the Black Suns, a loosely connected underground nativist cell. They're often called cosmological Nazis, holocaust deniers, even a Thelemic fighting creed! A couple of them are frequent visitors here. I can't name names, of course, but let's just say, they're two of the brightest lights on the far right, the intellectual leaders."

"How bright are we talking?"

"They've read their Guénon and Evola. They don't seem like terrible people. They just believe that modernisation is a vast process of general devolution. The collapse of natural hierarchies has led to shallow materialism, spiritual entropy and powerlessness. Man, after all, is not motivated by love, nor by noble ideas such as equality. He is primed to seek power."

"You're not a fascist, are you?"

"I certainly know a few, but I'm not racist, if that's what you mean. Call it naked self-interest, but I'm against bombing bookshops. I don't discriminate in terms of who I allow to sleep here, either. Nobody can sleep here, except me. Ha!"

Lester bristled, because he was just about to ask.

XLI

Later, when Anaïs and Lester were cosy in the incensed abyss, sipping their absinthe, Mike stroked his beard and wondered: "You came to Paris to look for Gérard Derenne and wound up here?"

"I never take the conventional route."

"Of course, he isn't somebody I think about often. Like most Parisians, I consciously avoid him. An artist friend of mine had a project a few years ago where he would sell magazines and newspapers exactly as they were, except with Gérard's articles—and all mentions of him—cut out. They were surprisingly popular. And come to think of it, prophetic, don't you think?"

Lester clutched the absinthe and nodded, aware now that his understanding of events had been superficial at best.

"As much as I am loathe to attach any more significance to him than he already claims to possess, doesn't it make you wonder if the carnage outside, the collapse of social discipline, might in some way be connected to his disappearance?"

"I had wondered that, yes," Lester said.

"Right, so it was assumed for many years that Gérard was the most powerful person in France, an intellectual monarch—unelected, unaccountable, essentially untouchable. One of the arguments in favour of kings, of course, is that they provide a more stable society."

"There's that old saying, Joni Mitchell, I think: you don't know what you've got till it's gone."

"Now I think about it, maybe this is going off on too much of a tangent, but have you done any research into the Fabian movement?"

"It rings a bell. I met some Philosophy students the other day, but I've lost that notebook. Anaïs, did I leave it at yours? Anaïs?"

"I don't know," she said, still dazed.

"Well I'm sure you know," Mike said, "the Fabians are a liberal conspiracy. Their whole project, going back to the early twentieth century, was to co-opt the labour and other supposedly progressive movements in favour of elite interests. They were founded, ironically enough, by Frank Podmore, who was also an influential member of the Society for Psychical Research, which investigated psychic phenomena. Rather like the Nazis, members such as Havelock Ellis were eugenicists. And just like those nasty, anti-egalitarian thugs I have already mentioned, HG Wells proposed turning the Fabians into society's official ruling order. The Fabians are also deeply connected to child sexual abuse and the intelligence community. They supported the Paedophile Information Exchange in the UK, a *progressive* organisation that campaigned for lowering the age of consent to four, or abolishing it completely, and counted Peter Hayman, the deputy director of MI6 and a child rapist, among its members. This has led to all kinds of conspiracies regarding a *Satanic* child-sex network involving politicians, although I must remain sceptical, because there isn't any evidence that they actually worshipped the devil. Either way, they and their members such as John Maynard-Keynes actually laid the groundwork for the synarchic state—or the New World Order—with the founding of global institutions such as the World Bank, the European Union and the Bilderberg Group, all of which Gérard attends, advises or supports."

At the mention of these names, Lester's attention waned. "I've actually become more interested in the Surrealists. Do you happen to know..."

"The Surrealists are interesting," Mike cut in. "Did you know that they were a Masonic society?"

"No." Lester stifled a yawn. "Why?"

"Have you noticed how the chess boards in many Surrealist paintings resemble the floors of Masonic lodges?"

"I'd never noticed it before."

"De Chirico and Ernst's work is littered with alchemical formulations, hidden allusions and codes that would be recognisable to the initiate, but invisible to the casual observer."

"I'm reading Breton's biography..."

"In Ernst's 1922 painting, 'A Friends' Reunion', Breton himself is wearing a red magician's cape and making what appears to be a Masonic hand signal!"

Mike showed Lester a print of the Ernst painting and gestured with his arm at a right angle, as Breton was in the group painting of the Surrealists.

"Even if Breton claimed that he was anti-theocratic, the Surrealists were still akin to a religious group with mystical inclinations. They had oaths of loyalty, excommunications, secret codes and rituals, daily café meetings with holy drinks, aperitifs. Think about the seances, the trances, Breton's celebration of Nadja's clairvoyant instincts. In his studio at 42 Rue Fontaine, Breton had a collection of voodoo masks and several copies of Agrippa's *Occult Philosophica*. The Pope of Surrealism must have harnessed occult powers, must he not? He practised a kind of mind control, or brainwashing, to instill loyalty to his *own* occult order of great men. Remember what he wrote in the first Manifesto? 'Surrealism will usher you into death, which is a secret society!' "

Flipping back the notepad he'd located in the inside pocket of his jacket, Lester noticed the invisible trails connecting everywhere he'd been in luminous day-glo colours...

XLII

"Also, did you know..." Mike was leaving to go fetch candles, but poked his head back around the door to announce that, "the next avant-garde movement after the Surrealists was the Lettrists, who were also a Masonic order, as were the Situationist International. Both of these groups were actually orders of the Kabbalah disguised as art movements, and received their funding from Tibet, the same source as the Hermetic Order of the Golden Dawn. And the Golden Dawn circles back to the Theosophical Society, which was reestablished in Germany, led by Rudolf Steiner and Grand Secretary Marie Sivers. The formation of the Mystica Aeterna and the OTO Ordo Templi Orientis, an offshoot of traditional Masonic orders, via the Theosophical Society, had as its highest gift the 9th degree, still at its crudest and most experimental stage, *sex magic*. Fast-forward to the 1930s and you will find the Russian mystic Maria de Naglowska conducting seminars in a Montparnasse café, demonstrating her sex magic techniques to personalities such as Julius Evola, Man Ray and—André Breton."

Finally out of breath, Mike left Lester with some rudimentary reading material so he could decide if he wanted to proceed to the first stage of initiation: *The Satanic Bible* by Anton LaVey, *Demons of the Flesh: a Guide to Left-hand Path Sex Magic* by Nikolas and Zeena Schreck, and an anthology of writing on Satanic black masses, including works by Crowley and Yeats, titled *Necromancers*.

Anaïs was sitting in the big upholstered chair, browsing through *An Encyclopedia of Witchcraft and Demonology* in silence.

In this light, with her hair brushed back, she resembled Dracula's daughter. Lester tickled her under the chin, and she said: "Lester, are you going to start practising witchcraft?"

"Only if you're up for it."

She smiled and nodded.

Lester and Anaïs nibbled magic mushrooms and helped themselves to absinthe while they read the material Mike had given them. When he came back a couple of hours later with incense and black candles, their minds were turned onto the darker energies.

"So Mike, do you offer black magic?"

"Crowley would be furious at this term." Mike lit the wicks, his skin now translucent in the eerie light. "All magic is equal, beyond good and evil. Magick is simply the art and science of causing change to occur in conformity with the will."

"Have you ever hexed anybody?"

"Yes, and I've been hexed."

"How did you find out you'd been hexed?"

"In a text message."

"Alright," Lester fumbled around in his wallet. "How much does it cost?"

"For a hex?"

"Yes."

"Financially, it will set you back three hundred euros, but you've got to be aware of the threefold return rule."

"What's that?"

"The damage you inflict will come back at you three times as hard."

"Can you do two for the price of one?"

"Considering the havoc you will be wreaking, a few hundred euros is a trivial investment for a hex."

"I only have two hundred."

Mike fixed his gaze on Lester's wretched material body, clearly the victim of some cosmic joke, a mental and moral weakling. "That depends, who are the victims?"

Lester whispered into the magician's ear.

"Excellent choices."

"Thank you. Can I be cheeky and add a third person?"

"Alright, but since you're making a smaller financial contribution, you have to perform some of the rites yourself."

"Deal."

XLIII

The ceremony opened with the Mystic, Mike, seating himself on a throne before a small brazier. Lester and Anaïs took their places on triangular stools at the points of the pentagram rug; at the clap of his hand, it lit up in red. They were dressed in robes with the cowls drawn down over their faces, and only their eyes visible through the narrow eye-slits. Clouds of incense hung about the room. When they were seated, the Mystic rose from his seat, and taking one of the swords from the brazier, held it pointing towards the altar, a coffee table painted with the symbols of the Tree of Life.

"Antay I was Malcooth-Vegabular,
Vegadura, ee-ar-la-ah moov."

Following this he stepped over to Lester, rested the point on his forehead, and uttered a further rigmarole, finishing with a loud shriek of, "Adonis!"

Then he went through an identical performance in front of Anaïs, except that to begin with he stood silently in front of her for a full minute, breathing deeply the while—breathing in the soul of their priestess...

Premilinaries over, the Mystic Mike proceeded to execute a variety of ecstatic dances. He lashed himself into an absolute frenzy, brandishing his sword, dancing and leaping around in the magic circle. His eyes blazed. The words he chanted had a compelling, monotonous and exotic rhythm, his eyes alight with fanatical enthusiasm.

"Thrill with lissom lust of the light,
O Man, my Man;
Come careening out of the night
To me, to me;
Come with Apollo in bridal dress...

"In sympathetic magic, items belonging to the victim are used as symbolic representations," Mike said. "And on the magic plane, symbols are living things. Do you possess any items belonging to your victims? Place them on the altar."

Lester took from his wallet three business cards and placed them on the coffee table-altar. Mike grabbed a stray cat from a box in his kitchenette and stuffed it into a sack, tying it with a rope. Lester, as he was to be the executioner, changed places with Mike.

Mike instructed Lester to take a Ghurka knife from its place and grasp the squirming sack. He untied it, drew forth the struggling and terrified cat, and held her with his left hand at arm's length above his head. In his right he held the knife with its point towards the brazier. The Mystic calmed the cat by dabbing ether on its nose. All was now ready for the sacrificial invocation, which was taken from the *Grimoires* of Aleister Crowley.

The Mystic gave Anaïs a bowl, and she held it underneath the cat to catch the blood. Lester severed through the cat's viscera and the blood dripped into the kidney-shaped vessel. His knees began to wobble, but he felt Mike's hand on his back to steady him for the remainder of the ritual.

Mike took the bowl from Anaïs, uttered a consecratory formula. Together they approached Lester. The Mystic flung back the cowl to reveal his face, pale and sweating, trying with all his might to remain standing. The Mystic dipped his finger in blood and drew a pentagram on Lester's glistening forehead. "*Ateh*." To Anaïs he turned next. Her attempts at stillness did not betray a fright that radiated from within her, little pants coming out of her downturned mouth. The Mystic painted her white forehead with the mark of Satan.

The Mystic poured the blood into a silver cup and handed it to Lester, who cupped it in his quivering hands. He took it between his lips and the swamp pooled down his throat, causing him to gag and splutter. The Mystic held a white cloth over his mouth and tipped his head back. He gave the cup a priestly wipe with the folded towel and handed it to Anaïs. She closed her eyes and took the cup, her black painted nails glistening, and tipped the blood into her mouth. As it disappeared, a part of herself also seemed to be eradicated, and she came back into the room, eyes widening, electrolised by dark energy.

"Now we have performed our preliminary rites," Mike said, "we must add the essential fuel to any ritual. Do you know the force of which I speak, Lester?"

"Breton said, 'Desire is the great force.'"

"Good. Lester, do you desire this woman?"

"I do."

"Anaïs, do you desire this man?"

She stared ahead, gulping the remnants of blood in her throat.

"Anaïs, are you okay?" Lester asked.

"Yes," she said.

"Good," the Magician bowed his head. "Anaïs, reveal your vulva to him, so that he can see you are God."

"I think she's on the blob."

"In *The Book of the Law*, Crowley writes, 'The best blood is of the moon, monthly,'" Mike said. "The lunar path is open, Lester."

If they were to have adhered to the strict training of the Ordo Templi Orientis, Lester should have first completed seven *chakras* before encountering the eighth degree of initiation—masturbatory worship with mental projections at the moment of orgasm. Only then would he be instructed in the techniques of the ninth degree, the transmutation of reproductive energy with a female daemon. But time was of the essence, and Mike assured Lester that these rites were proven to work with novices under the guidance of a grand master. It was not, after all, a matter of personality, but Energy.

Back beside the altar, the two initiates waited rapt for the emergence of some presence, their clammy hands clasped together. Mike brought the needle down on Wagner's *Parsifal*. These dark hymns, he explained, were the favoured mood music for sex rites of the OTO. Anaïs was relieved of her cloak and laid down on the altar next to the sigil cards. Mike dabbed her nose with ether to relax her and Lester rubbed her with holy ointments, his hands paying particular attention to her erogenous zones while the tempestuous pipes of Wagner cascaded. Her breath intensified as Lester kissed her gently at first, then began to sink his teeth into her neck. He felt like the embodiment of the Beast who was imbued with a newfound Power, awake to his libidinous strengthening as something more than just a casual itch or urge, but an earthly Calling. What was it that called him? Some latent Will that had broken through his conscious mind from deep within his pelvis, a reservoir of riches that rose in level. He undid his belt buckle and pulled her creamy white legs towards him, eyes fixed on the tunnel to the astral plane. Behind Anaïs, the Magus, hooded, repeated a poem:

> "Will reigns Omnipotent;
> Love lieth at the Foundation."

Lester entered Anaïs smoothly and held himself inside her, blood squelching. Mike lay his hands on her head and instructed her to suck the light from Lester. Lodged inside her with his eyes closed, it took a great deal of Will to keep from releasing his Power. "I'm going to cum," he said more than once.

"No!" the Mystic instructed him. "If you feel you are about to, pull out." And so he did, and Anaïs giggled at the Power she wielded over him.

With his eyes closed, he was returned to prehistoric times. The universe began when a huge block of cosmic ice somehow encountered the sun. A flood through which Zeus destroyed the world. Could there have been any event in the earth's history catastrophic enough to cause flooding of large areas of the whole globe? Mike fanned a tarot deck, and Lester chose a card. The Hanged Man card... his feet are planted in heaven and whose head only touches earth, the free and immolated adept, the revealer menaced with death...

> "And I heard a voice which spoke to me:
> Behold, this is the man who has seen the Truth
> No suffering such as no earthly fortune can ever cause."

The Hanged Man is a disciple who has been hung upside down at a certain stage in his initiation. Gold tumbles out of his pockets. He has not really given up on the world and is in great spiritual danger. He saw embers of his sword in a fire, and he felt the jolting of the hills beneath him as he rode through the sky on a ram.

He heard the *Book of the Law*, dictated by the voice of Aiwass, in Cairo. Was this just a schizophrenic episode, as voices from the left ear often denote? Or was Aiwass one of the Secret Chiefs said to govern the planet, similar to the *mahatmas* in Theosophical lore or the *bodhisattvas* in the Buddhist left-hand path? Crowley believed it was a contact with a higher Intelligence, and Crowley himself had become a prophet, the Aeon of Horus, the new age that would replace all the old religions with a higher mode of consciousness, and he was thereby installed as the Theosophical Great Man or World Teacher, charged with the spiritual supervision of the planet. He believed he was a religious figure of the same stature as Christ, Buddha and the prophet Mohammed. Buddha condensed his teaching to *Anetta*, Christ to Agape (Love), Crowley, Thelema (Will)... The Mystic presented Lester with a gargling toad representing Christ, and Lester bit its head off.... The overcoming of inner and external sexual boundaries, the reconstruction of the self through trespass and inversion, the integration and acceptance of the horrifying aspects of the *maya*; all of these Crowleyan methods would be immediately familiar to the more radical practitioners of the left-hand path, such as the Aghori. Just as the Indian left-hand path Kapalikas deliberately dishonoured themselves in the eyes of the legitimate Brahmin society as a tool of transcendence, one could make a case for Crowley's deliberate provocation of the acceptable standards of his time as a pure expression of one of the sinister current's most important methods. The remanifestation of a rich, respectable, Cambridge-educated scion of a devout Christian family into the "Wickedest Man in the World," a destitute junkie expelled from several countries and calumnied as the foulest of perverts in the international press may have been Aleister Crowley's most effective magical act!

As she proceeded to swallow Lester with her ecstatic shuddering, his Will was directed more and more towards the object of the operation, his daemonic female companion, and he fell into a blackout. His ego consciousness was abolished; he stopped only when the blood of the Red Lion was one with the Gluten of the White Eagle, and the serpent and the egg had fused completely. The result of this fusion is called the Elixir, and perfect simultaneity of the two beings was harmonised in the mantra, recited by the Magus:

"Jungiter in vati vates: rex inclyte Hermes to venius, verba nefanda ferens."
("Behold! The priest is jouned to the priest! Illustriuous kind of the Staff mayest though come, Hermes, bearing unutterable words!")

Lester knelt down and cupped his lips to her genital cavern. He sucked the bloody cocktail of coagulated ovarian semen into his mouth and gargled with it. O, cake of light! Mike had laid the talismen on Anaïs's chest, and he dribbled the mixture onto the cards belonging to his victims. Onto an unfurled poster, Lester slapped a scooped handful of the red snot. They took paintbrushes and smeared the mark of Satan onto the pristine visage of the philosopher. The two men's eyes locked as they desecrated the image, their thought forms projecting dark power onto the body of the astral corpse.

XLV

Lester and Anaïs walked to Père Lachaise cemetery with sirens warping the thick black air, the marks of Satan still on their foreheads, a trickle of blood running down her thigh. The acid tab had started to hit him. Temporal space was crushed by giant mechanical hands. In five days, not only his mind but his appearance had changed as one might expect over the course of five years. In the reflection of a car window, when he removed his fedora he saw above the shiner Badbeger had given him that his hair was clumped thicker in the centre of his forehead; he seemed to be losing it at the temples. With her ragamuffin mop and lymphatic shuffle always one step behind him, Anaïs appeared to have been yanked backwards by those same big hands, as if on a pair of child's reins. The blood ran back up her leg as she dabbed it with a tissue. She looked as though she belonged to something other than the terrestrial world, where almost everything bored or scared her.

Bats swooped above them as he led her along crooked paths of Père Lachaise through memorial slabs. The ruins of dead aristocratic poets, vampires and Freemasons were laid out in some vast cosmological design, as if they corresponded somehow to the stars sparkling in the black firmament.

By intuition alone, he located the black gravestone of Raymond Roussel—another surrealist genius who was ridiculed in his lifetime—and decided that this was the place to sit down, roll a joint, and consider.

Anaïs had been eager to join him on a journey into the twilight zone. They had now gone too far to turn back, and now she had shut herself down into the dark mode of silence? Humidity burst from his pores.

"What are you thinking, Anaïs?"
Anaïs stared ahead into the darkness of the graveyard.
"Anaïs? Please say something."
For every thousand words he had spoken on the walk across

town, she had barely spoken one. "I feel so fake," she said finally. "Nobody knows who I am. Not really."

"There's a difference between how other people perceive you and how you really are?"

She blinked, yes.

He coddled her, kissed her head, but she seemed locked into her own mental projection room. "What's the difference? What are we not seeing? What are you thinking?"

Cloaked figures approached them, tombstones glowing. Martinists, Theosophists, Symbolists, Decadents, Oscar Wilde, Apollinaire, Jim Morrison huddled and danced, their robes swirling into the distance, beyond the walls of the cemetery and into the city.

"Please speak." Time stretched and echoed in the silence. "We've set off into the graveyard together. I don't mind navigating most of the time, but you're going to have to read the map when we get lost sometimes. Because I don't know what I'm doing either. I'm losing my sanity too."

After another symphony of city silence, a tear burst through her frosty white pallor. Anaïs said, "Do you believe in the Self?"

"I may have only realised over the last few days, but I don't think I am one person. I am nobody. I am somebody. I am several people."

"You're a liar?"

"No. I tell the truth. I just tell it wearing different costumes."

"So it's all an act?"

"Do you like Inspector Maigret?"

"He's okay. I don't understand your obsession with him."

"Maybe you'll like this one. There's a great observation in a Maigret story about a brain surgeon. At the end, Maigret finally meets his intellectual equivalent. This man behaves in such a lofty, detached manner towards everybody. Finally, Maigret takes a puff on his cigar and says: 'It is rare to encounter people who do not play a role, even when they are alone. Most men feel the need to watch themselves living, to listen to themselves speaking. Not him. He was himself, fully himself, and he did not bother to hide his feelings.'"

Anaïs, with her obsessive self-reflections and doubts, her fixation on what Laing called "ontological insecurity," sighed at the fortitude of such a personality. "Do you know anybody like that?"

"I only know one. We lived together at university. A soldier by the name of Mushroom Daley. He was such a convincing person, so whole and unaffected, so consistent in every way, he seemed unreal."

"When did you see him last? I'd like to meet him, ask how he does it."

"Yesterday, before the blast. He arrived and then he vanished, just like that."

Raymond Roussel's tombstone was deep black marble, a reverse portal into the night sky with the stars removed. Lester tipped his hat off, lay back on it and began to question whether these were really his thoughts, or those he had been programmed to believe. Was he brainwashing Anaïs?

He felt a hand on his face. When he opened his eyes, Anaïs's wide, lunar face was shining above him. "What are you thinking, Lester?"

"I've come to the conclusion that it doesn't matter what you think of yourself. You are the impression you make on others. You can become a different person to different people."

"Like schizophrenia?"

"In the 21st Century, a schizoid personality can be an asset. Be the person you need to be to get ahead."

She lay down next to him on the marble, and he wondered if the stars she saw were the same ones he saw, and concluded that it didn't matter. Over time, he would learn to see the world through her eyes—at least when he squinted.

"I'm going to say something, and if you feel like it, I invite you to repeat it." He turned her face towards his. "I love you."

"I love you too."

They kissed.

XLVII

"Can I do anything for you?"
"I don't think you can help if I'm having a bad trip about you."
"What's that supposed to mean?"
"Don't take it personally."
They had climbed out of the cemetery and were trying to navigate the traffic, but the streets were flooded with blasts of red and green light. Anaïs, who had licked an acid tab off his tongue as they were lying down on Raymond Roussel's grave, spoke as if not to another human being, but some Other she had composed from her Catholic superstitions, hallucinations, and her beloved psychiatry books.

"You're a nightmare," she said. "I'm genuinely afraid of you."
"How can you say you love somebody who gives you nightmares?"
"Fear. It's attractive and addictive."
"But what are you afraid of?"
"You knowing too much about me."
"Do you think I'm a danger to you or I'm trying to hurt you?"
"Not necessarily hurt me, but laugh at me."
"I laugh at everybody. What is it?"
"You'd kill me and publicly embarrass me if I told you."
"It's insulting to suggest that I would reveal a secret."
"I thought that was your job."
He had to laugh at that one. There were no cabs forthcoming, no matter how much he waved.

"If you told me you'd murdered somebody in cold blood, I wouldn't judge you or tell anybody."
"I wouldn't mind telling you I murdered someone."
"I'm struggling to think of anything I would judge you for."
"Things you judge everyone for."
"I can't think of anything."
"You talk about it all the time."
"Gérard? I'm over him. Badbeger? I don't care if you did. Honestly."

"Neither."

"Bestiality? Did you fuck your cat? When I was a virgin, I used to think my cat's tongue would feel nice."

"No, no, no."

"Gimme a clue. This is killing me."

She turned and looked at him. The familiarity of lovers had not quite gone. But he was a specimen to her, a dangerous predator. "One of my friends spent three months in a mental institution after working for *Down N Out!*"

"You're not working for *Down N Out!* You're with me. In fact, we're not even working."

"Yesterday, before the... thing..."

"The ritual?"

"Yes, my friend text me to say she believes that drug addicts are habitual liars and intelligent, manipulative cunts. Like all the other people in your world."

"You reckon I'm in the same category?"

"I think you may be but maybe not as radically as them."

"I'm worried that you're going to accuse me of some more bad shit," Lester said. "Even worse than what's already out there."

"I don't want to ruin your life."

"But you think I've done some bad shit?"

"You think of yourself as a terrible human being. You are evil."

"Maybe I'm deluded," Lester sighed, "but I have taken you under my wing, encouraged and invited you to do something exciting with me. It hasn't worked out, but I've been there for you when you needed it."

"Yes, you are deluded. I need a break from that."

"How is that deluded?"

"It's not a romantic relationship, being under the wing."

"I offered you opportunities. I liked your style. Your aura."

"I never cared about opportunities."

Through the tears in his eyes, he struggled to see the screen on his phone. The map was one big necropolis. "I'm confused, Anaïs, and a little hurt. You accuse me of being delusional, a nightmarish figure...."

"I am possessed by the devil."

"I can't tell if you're being serious or melodramatic."

"I really believe it. I think I need an exorcism."

"There's no such thing as the devil."

"You just performed a rite to Satan!"

"Not all Satanists believe in the devil. It's a metaphor for sin, transgression, pleasure."

"What if I'm possessed by you, Lester?"

He tried to imagine what he might look like to her now. His incisors protruded downward into his lower lip. He tasted blood in his mouth. To have influenced somebody a little is a great feat, but to have driven them insane could be regarded as even more impressive...

XLVIII

They took a cab to the Hotel du Nord, the location of the Marcel Carné film. His tie was skewed, they clutched each other in a forlorn manner and took the keys to room number sixteen. They had a simple divan with French windows overlooking the bridge on the quai. At the balcony, Lester hugged her from behind while she smoked. "Without your love, I'd be nothing."

He told her there had been so many times over the last week when he regretted not only coming to Paris, but ever leaving his village. It would have saved him so much anxiety to have stayed in the East Midlands and never gone to London, let alone Paris. Anaïs cut such a glamorous figure in chiaroscuro, he felt ashamed and dirty for not only inducting her into this world, but for pretending that he had come here for any reason other than to be with her.

By the time he had taken his clothes off and laid down beside her, she was already frozen in sleep.

SATURDAY

XLIX

As he lay there bolt awake, teeth clamped together, reading Georges Bataille with his *gamine* asleep next to him, Lester conceived of himself in a glass bed, under glass sheets. And not only was he sleeping under glass, but he himself felt like he was painfully transparent, unable to keep his heart from coming out of his mouth. Had she known, Anaïs might have been uneasy to discover that she had undergone a drastic transformation in his mind, from woman to symbol.

Anaïs was what Bataille had described as a "bird of ill omen." Everything about her—her sleepwalker's gait, her tone of voice, her ability to spread a kind of silence around her, her hunger for sacrifice, helped give the impression of a contract she might have drawn up with death. A life like hers could only make sense among men who were doomed to misery.

L

Lester unattached himself from his bird, her shadow, on the wet sheets. On the balcony of the Hotel du Nord, he smoked a joint, appreciated the vibrancy of the early morning colours, still heightened in the acid afterglow. The linden trees by Canal Saint-Martin were fulsome and bursting with doves. The birdsong was so pleasant and chirrupy, he threw his arms out as though he was conducting it.

Water rushed through the mechanical lock. Curtains in the windows opposite were shaking open. Bowls of coffee were being prepared to be dipped with fresh bread he could smell from the bakery.

The city was waking up.

Lester knew his friend was on the early morning shift back in Wales. He imagined him at his desk, peering through misty sunlight, keeping an eye on the sheep in the field.

"Les, how you doing?"

"Really good, brother. It's magical here."

"That's really good to hear. I was worried about you."

"No need to worry, brother." Lester took another toke on the joint. "I'm on top of the world."

"I'm glad you've found some peace. I don't suppose you want to know what's happening back in the British media."

"What harm will it do?"

"It's not all rosy over here, I have to warn you."

"Hit me, I'm ready."

"Hugh Woolley's been dispatched to Paris to cover your beat."

Lester's chest tensed. He clutched the railing, as he had nowhere to pace around. "Hugh Woolley? Is his mum driving him again?"

"Hold on, let me check social media. He updated his feed seven minutes ago. They've just arrived at Dover in the car, about to cross the channel. They should be in Paris by evening at the latest."

"I could have done a great job on this story. And I might still yet. Maybe I should call Sizebank..."

"That's the other thing I ought to tell you, Les."

"Go on."

"I wouldn't call Sizebank if I were you, nor anybody at *Down N Out!*"

"Do they still hate me that much?"

"Maybe more. It's hard to tell."

"Why? What's happened? I can tell by your voice..."

Tom was used to breaking bad news. This was something he should brace himself for. "Sizebank had a terrible accident."

Lester had foggy memories of the magician's house, and hoped it was just an astral projection. "How terrible?"

"He was already injured, wasn't he?"

"He had a yoga accident they tried to blame me for."

"They were moving office, weren't they?" Perkins sighed. "Downsizing. He'd forgotten his last box of trainers. The removal van was parked across the street. He couldn't look both ways because his neck was in a brace. So he walked straight into oncoming traffic."

It was uncanny. Lester remembered seeing something to this effect at the height of his passion.

"A number 55 bus flattened him. Broke both arms and legs. Permanent spinal damage. He's currently in a controlled coma."

Lester ran into the bathroom and heaved a psychedelic swirl of green absinthe and menstrual blood into the sink.

LI

Lester inhaled half of Paris's water supply from the tap, grabbed Anaïs in her slumber, told her it was time to check out of the hotel. Turned against the wall in a thick coat, she didn't respond. He shook her violently, turned her over to face him. Her eyes rolled down from the ceiling of her skull.

"It... didn't... work?"

"What didn't? It absolutely worked." She slumped back into the drool on her pillow. "Anaïs, what's up?"

"The drugs. I took them."

"Didn't we both? Now get up, it's time to leave."

"The... other... drugs." She flung her arm in the direction of her bag on the floor. From the look of the squeezed pack, she'd finished off her anti-psychotics as well as a strip of his anti-depressants.

"Oh, sweet Satan."

He dashed to the bathroom, filled a glass full of water, threw it over her. She unpeeled herself from the bed, then slumped back down on the dry half. "Get up, we're leaving." He stood her up, held her warm, white face. Her eyes were out of focus, staring beyond him, into the past.

He hadn't any experience with overdoses, except he knew most pharmaceuticals are only fatal when mixed with alcohol. By their standards, they hadn't drunk that much yesterday. There was still a chance she could walk it off.

He paid with an expired bank card, dragged her around the streets, distracting her with breakfast items: strawberry tarts, lemon mousses in bakery windows. Told her he'd buy her anything she wanted, just get some sugar in the blood. But she was as unresponsive as a frozen pudding.

Back at the Cyrano for a coffee, while he figured out what to do, there was the same old man who'd been there on Friday, playing solitaire:

"Look who it is. I was hoping you might come back." He pulled some more old glossy magazines out of a plastic bag. "You know who's featured in this month's *Factor X*?"

Lester recalled the publication now, the one that had been blown up in the blast.

"Gérard Derenne."

"What are the chances?"

"Don't talk to me about chance, young man. There is no such thing!"

Gulp. "There isn't?"

"Weren't you here yesterday talking about Breton, and his belief in petrifying chance and coincidence?"

"I don't remember."

"Carl Jung called it synchronicity. Even in the 1950s, he knew there was enough evidence in science to account for the acausal combination of events. Look here, allow me to demonstrate. In front of me there are five cards turned face down. Two of them are marked with an X on the other side. Would you care to pick a card?"

Despite his impatience, Lester hovered his hands over the cards and snapped one from the table. Sure enough, it was marked with an X.

"Young lady, would you care to pick a card?"

Anaïs stared blankly ahead of her.

"She's not feeling well. We're actually on our way to the hospital."

"Well in that case, I beg your pardon. Here, take the magazine. Read the article about Gérard. Quite an eye-opener. Get well soon, young lady."

Lester ushered Anaïs out of the café and ordered them a cab.

LII

From the back of a cab on the Champs-Élysées, Lester saw a familiar mane of orange hair. In a slutty nightdress, Ridicula Goodman was flogging *Down N Out!* to cars stuck in the traffic. "*Down N Out! Down N Out!*" Her fall from grace, and subsequent humiliation as a lowly street vendor, was filmed by cameramen. Was this some unconscious prank, a trick of cosmology? Anaïs looked utterly abject and withdrawn, as though her soul had been pecked away at, devoured. Lester slid down the seat, hyperventilating, as he imagined how abysmal his fate would be, given the threefold return rule.

LIII

When they arrived at the emergency department, the nurse couldn't say if Anaïs would be seen in an hour or a day's time. He didn't know if the police would be called to arrest him, or if he too would be certified insane. While they waited to be examined, he had time to take stock of his relationship with her, how his infatuation with her—and the negative effect their relationship had on her health—was almost identical to Breton and Nadja.

She too had begun by sending him correspondence, often decorated by strange drawings. One featured a "symbolic portrait" of Lester, as a lion whose tail ensnared that of a mermaid Anaïs. Another represented "the Lover's Flower," made of two hearts and a pair of eyes, and bore the message: "You must be very busy at the moment? Send a few words to your Anaïs." She told Lester he was her "master": "If you desired it, for you I would be nothing, or merely a footprint." As neutrally as possible, Lester had noted that "in every sense of the word, she takes me for a god, she thinks of me as the sun." Like a chemical reaction, the contact between the unstable waif and the acidic theoretician produced one of the Surrealist revolution's most durable, and potent, weapons...

But almost immediately, Anaïs's "eccentricities" had darkened into serious aberration. She had written in her notebook: "It's raining still / My room is dark / Heart in the abyss / My sanity is dying..."

Late on Saturday afternoon, in the emergency department, she was diagnosed with schizophrenia.

Reading the biography, he noted how Breton had never visited Nadja during her internment in the Paris area (although it seems that Aragon and Eluard did), and quickly eliminated her from his conversation. If nothing else, Lester aspired to be a better man than Breton in this regard.

LIV

Running out of ideas and getting increasingly anxious in the hospital waiting room, an advert in *Factor X* magazine convinced Lester that treatment at a private institute outside Paris would be better than a psychiatric ward in a public hospital. In a state of desperation, as an absolute last resort, he called his parents for the first time in months and borrowed some money to get them the hell out of there.

In the back of another cab, he clutched Anaïs's soft, white hand. She had wrapped her head in a white cloth like a nun's habit and shivered.

A radio report said the security services now believed the bookshop bomb had been a "false flag" operation. The newly launched French edition of Barkbite News had leaked tapes showing white men in Islamic dress carrying backpacks onto the Left Bank shortly before the blast.

Lester and Anaïs were held up in traffic where groups of protesters had appeared on the Rue de Rivoli and were setting off flares that appeared to be torching the long commercial street's arcades. They turned the corner to Théâtre du Châtelet and Théâtre de la Ville, hosting Gérard's month-long immersive reproduction of the French Revolution. It had been going on for three weeks already. Now there was no point wishing he had attended for the sake of his story. His only concern now was Anaïs's wellbeing, getting her out of the city that was driving them both mad.

Some of the audience were on the balcony of the Châtelet, sipping champagne and taking photographs. Because outside the theatre, a more gripping event was happening. A flat-bed truck was parked opposite the theatre, and a mob had surrounded it, raising clubs, garden rakes and devil's pitchforks.

"Occult or secret knowledge is the basis for all power in human society!" boomed a voice from the mobile stage.

Lester leaned his head out the window, but couldn't see who was speaking.

"In nature, you will observe that camouflage is universal among predators and victims alike! Blossoms imitate fragrances and colours which their objects of desire find attractive. Dogs bark and feign attack on enemies of whom they are, in fact, terrified. Likewise, men proclaim their altruism, or their love of truth, while they selfishly scramble for personal advantage!"

The thugs set off more flares, casting a red mist across the square. Cars blared their horns, trying to manoeuvre out of the jam. Lester wound the window back down to protect them, as he was getting increasingly anxious about the revolutionary spectacle that seemed to be synchronised with the one going on in his mind. Cops rammed through the traffic and parked a row of vans in front of the Théâtre de la Ville to prevent it from being stormed, but given the numbers in the crowd, it looked futile.

An image of the Pope was projected onto the front of the theatre by the protesters, who had taken control of the square and hijacked the projector.

"Driver, get us out of here as fast as you can, I'll pay you double," Lester yelped. "Something's going down here and I don't want to be a part of it. Do you agree, Anaïs?"

Eyes clenched tight, she nodded her head. "Go, just go, please!"

"Monsieur, madame, I will do what I can!"

"We see visible rulers claiming to be representatives of God," the voice outside Châtelet boomed, as a portrait of King Louis IV splashed against the facade, followed by the current president of France, "or the material forces of history. By embracing deception, our Leader has fashioned the ultimate system yet devised for the secure exercise of power!"

Gérard's face smacked against the theatre.

Lester and Anaïs's cab swerved through the traffic, knocking over hoodlums who slid across the bonnet and hurled abuse at them. "Go, just go!" Lester screamed. Tears ran down Anaïs's face. He pulled her close to him. "Ram the sons of bitches, I don't care! This is an emergency."

To Anaïs, he tried to talk reassuringly, but couldn't find any appropriate words, so wound up humming into her ear to drown out the noise of the raging battle. Soon he was singing to her, sobbing, wailing into hear headscarf, rocking side to side: "Baa, baa, black sheep, have you any wool? Yes, sir, yes, sir, three bags full. Know that song? Know that song, Anaïs? Come on, stay with me. Sing along. Baa, baa, black sheep, have you any wool? Yes, sir, yes sir, three bags full."

They were crossing the Seine when the mob stormed the theatre and the rozzers waded in, crashing the protesters over the head with eels. Anaïs and Lester wailed, as though it was their own skulls that were being cracked.

LV

The sun was setting over the forest when their driver rolled through the gates to the hospital. Huge lawns were sprung with Salvador Dali sculptures of melted clocks. Patients dressed in folk costumes were playing croquet with marble spheres decorated like eyeballs. An electrolised black cat skulked around the patio of the big country house, shocking inmates. Immediately upon arrival, Anaïs was put in a luxurious room with a double bed and window looking out onto the beautiful grounds with woods and lake. "Do you think they let lovers sleep together here?" Lester asked.

"Maybe," she deadpanned, staring at the ceiling.

"Do you want me to get you anything?"

"Some fags."

He said he'd try and find the shop, but this hospital wasn't like any other he'd been to. It seemed to have been designed by the insane, with a view to inducing paranoia. Down the long corridor, posters disturbed his mind:

THE CONTINUOUS, CINEMATIC-STYLE EXPERIENCE OF REALITY IS AN ILLUSION CREATED BY OUR NERVOUS SYSTEMS!

TO ACCELERATE OUT OF 3RD DIMENSIONAL EXPERIENCE, YOU NEED *THE* NON-DIMENSIONAL ENERGY: YOU NEED TACHYON ENERGY!

PARANORMAL EXPERIENCES OF NURSES IN HOSPITALS

THE RELEVANCE OF PAST LIVES: TALK TO SOMEBODY WHO UNDERSTANDS

THE POSITIVE EFFECT OF MUSIC ON THE BLOOD

At least it seemed like there was plenty for the nutters to do here, like get involved in "worker democracy." Although Anaïs was one of the laziest creatures he had ever known—maybe it would improve her work ethic, make her more useful on future jobs, if she ever recovered, which was of course the priority.

A stout German doctor with an electrolysed haircut, wearing a lab coat over a denim shirt and corduroys, approached Lester while he was flailing around, lost. "Looking for a smoke?"

"Yes!"

"Follow me."

So this really was an unusual hospital.

They passed a room filled with rows and rows of shellac boxes the size of toilet cubicles. A pretty young female patient, stark naked, opened one of the doors and exited with a healthy glow. "Good evening, Dr Reich."

"How much do you know about our work?"

"Not a lot. Are you licensed?"

"The Orgone Institute was opened in 1957 and does not exist in any official sense." They shook hands. Lester felt somewhat calmer now, having escaped the nightmare of Paris, but was still teetering on the edge of emotional collapse, unsure if he had done the right thing in bringing them to this strange, unknown place that seemed like it could be just another alien, totalised system of distress.

"My girlfriend has been diagnosed with schizophrenia. She thinks she's possessed by the devil, and I am the devil."

At the mention of "schizophrenia," Reich grimaced.

Through the window, Lester saw a man dressed as Napoleon unrobe, then enter one of the shellac cubicles sheltered by a pagoda. "What are the boxes?" Lester wanted to know. "Are they saunas? Time machines?"

LVI

Back in her room, Anaïs was still rigid in a full-length dark coat, her head covered in the white hanky. Reich approached her as though she was a rare mineral or gem—with empathy and awe.

"Your fear of the cosmos is justified, or at least understandable," Dr Reich said. "Most people who deviate from a well-trodden path may easily become lunatics. If you do not understand the infinity of which your thoughts and deeds are part, you can go to pieces."

One of Anaïs's great attractions was that you never quite knew what she was thinking, but that was also what made her distress so unknowable, and therefore frightening. She blinked. Lester perched on the bed and held her pinkie. "She seems suspended all alone in her own private world, doc."

"Don't worry, son. In addition to my work with Freud, I have studied astronomy, electronics, Planck's quantum theory and Einstein's theory of relativity. I have never for one moment escaped the feeling of the magnitude of the universe. The fantasy of being suspended all alone in the universe is more than a fantasy of the maternal womb. Psychoanalytic theory states that in the insane, the unconscious breaks through into consciousness. The patient thus loses the barrier against the chaos of her own unconscious as well as the ability to test reality in the world outside herself. In the schizophrenic, the mental breakdown is ushered in by the phantasy, in one form or another, that the world is coming to an end."

Lester saw a glimmer of mutual fear in Anaïs's eyes.

"I was deeply moved by the earnestness with which Freud tried to understand the insane. He towered like a mountain above the conceited and conventional opinions on mental disease held by the psychiatrists of the old school. This or the other was 'crazy', they said; and that was that. When, as a medical student, I became acquainted with the questionnaire for mental patients, I felt ashamed. I wrote a little play in which I pictured the desperation of the mental patient who cannot master the surging life forces in himself and who looks for help and clarity. Consider the stereotypes of a catatonic patient, such movements as steadily pressing a finger against her forehead, as if in an effort to think; or the deep, searching, far-away look of these patients. And then the psychiatrist asks: 'How old are you?' 'What is your name?' 'How much is 3 x 6?' "

Lester nodded in recognition of their experience at the previous hospital.

"The Steinhof in Vienna contained around 20,000 crazy people. Each one had felt his world tumbling down, and, in order to hold onto something, had created an imaginary world in which they could exist. The outer world and its infinite stimuli can be nothing but a chaos, a chaos of which the sensations from its own body are a part. *The ego and the outer world are experienced as a unity.*"

Lester looked outside at the croquet players tapping the eyeballs around the lawn and smiled, reassured. Dr Reich might be a genius.

"Stimuli from the outer world may then be perceived as inner experiences, or conversely, inner perceptions may be experienced as coming from the outer world. In some cases a patient may believe themselves to be persecuted with electricity by an obscure enemy, whereas in reality she only perceives her own bio-electric currents. Back then, I knew nothing of the reality of bodily sensations in mental patients. Nevertheless, it was the nucleus of my conviction that the beginning of the loss of reality testing in schizophrenia lies in the patient's misinterpretation of the sensations arising from her own body."

"Doctor, can I speak to you for a minute?"

Reich seemed annoyed by the patient's partner, usually a hindrance to the therapeutic process, if not the cause. He took Lester into the corridor and tapped a Lucky Strike out of the pack for him. "What is it?"

"I'm not sure she's a schizophrenic. It seems to have happened too suddenly."

"It is my belief that most psychological and physical illnesses have a sexual causation." Lester blushed. "It took me years to convince my colleagues to adopt the term 'sex-economy' to describe our work here. And you must be aware that our methods, while more effective than state hospitals, do not have a hundred-percent success rate. In fact, the only way mental ailments can ever be cured, in our opinion, is for society itself to come to terms with the sexual process."

"What do you propose for her, doc?"

"Be frank with me. Are you sexual partners?"

"We've slept together a couple of times."

Lester felt himself shrinking.

"Psychic health depends on orgiastic potency. The capacity to surrender in the sexual act. Mental illness is the result of a disturbance in the natural capacity for love. In the case of orgiastic impotence, for which a vast majority of humans suffer, biological energy is dammed up, and this becomes the source of all kinds of irrational behaviour..."

"Wait," something bizarre occurred to him. "Are you saying that I can cure mental illnesses with my penis?"

"That's one way of looking at it."

"That's a lot of responsibility."

"But it's not necessarily *your* responsibility."

Lester inspected the doctor's expression for lewdness. His tanned features gave nothing away, except a love of the outdoors.

"Let me ask you another question. Is her family religious?"

"Catholic."

"Why am I not surprised?" Reich shook his head.

"What was it André Breton said: 'Believing in God is the equivalent of killing yourself. Faith is a form of suicide.' "

"Quite! And her father, was there any abuse in the family?"

"When I tried to tickle her, she said, 'it doesn't work if you were beaten as a child.' I don't know if there's any more to it. She doesn't share much."

"When a person is brought up in an atmosphere which negates life and sex, they acquire a pleasure anxiety. Pleasure anxiety is the soil on which the individual recreates the life-negating ideologies which are the basis of dictatorships. Morality's aim is to produce acquiescent subjects who are adjusted to the authoritarian order," Reich continued. "The family is the authoritarian state in miniature.

Men and women's authoritarian structure is basically produced by the embedding of sexual inhibitions and fear in their lives. When sexuality is prevented from attaining natural gratification, owing to the process of sexual repression, what happens is that it seeks various kinds of substitute gratifications. Natural aggression is distorted into brutal sadism, which constitutes the basis for imperialistic wars. The sexual effect of a uniform, the erotically provocative effect of rhythmically executed goose-stepping, the exhibitionistic nature of militaristic procedures, have been more practically comprehended by fashion designers than by our most erudite politicians, even though politicians subconsciously exploit this sexual content."

LVII

"May I ask you a more general question?" Lester said. "Do you think they're ready for Derenne to come and take back control?"
"Sorry, who?"
"Gérard Derenne. I was reading an article in the magazine where I found your clinic. It said all the chaos—the bombs, the protests, the confusion and panic—is something he has been anticipating, or even orchestrating, with the help of Roman Polanski and Steve Renault..."
"I know very little of this man, as we barely read the news here, and actually discourage our patients from consuming it. But from a limited knowledge, I would say that a ruler's mass psychological impact has to proceed from the presupposition that a führer, or the champion of an idea, can be successful only if his character bears a resemblance to the average individual. This philosopher fellow seems to stir the libido, particularly among reactionary women, and he seems to project an image of both liberty and authority—very powerful symbols in mass psychology. I hear he also has a lot of money and controls the media. So who knows? But that's enough of politics. Let's go and see your girlfriend."
Back in Anaïs's room, Reich traced the outline of her body with his hands, like a carnival magician about to saw her in half.
"All my patients are genitally disturbed. They must become genitally healthy. That means we must find and destroy all pathological attitudes which prevent the establishment of orgiastic potency. But in order to establish orgiastic potency, it is not sufficient to liberate the existing genital inhibitions or repressions. Sexual energy is bound up in the symptoms. I have developed the technique of character-analytic vegetotherapy. Its fundamental principle is the restoration of bio-psychic motility by means of dissolving rigidities—otherwise known as 'armour'—of the character and the musculature."
"What will this entail?" Lester frowned.
"My students and I will be conducting various kinds of

psychoanalysis and body-work on her. Don't be alarmed, it is a clinical technique that combines psychotherapy with breathing exercises and massage."

In case they wouldn't let him stay, he wrote his phone number in his notebook, ripped it out, gave it to Anaïs.

"That won't be necessary," Reich said. "Come with me, please."

Reich stroked Anaïs on the head like a cat and took them to a sheltered patio area with a dozen of the giant boxes in a line. It had an unusual aura of eerie calm. A mass of human activity still hummed in the atmosphere, but was not visible. A pretty young student in a floral peasant dress was acting as an usher to the paddock lined with benches and clothes pegs.

"What happens inside the boxes, professor?" Lester asked more sternly this time. He wouldn't leave her here before he had an answer.

The "nurse," who looked like she belonged at Woodstock rather than at a hospital, hushed him. "Keep your voice down. Patients are undergoing therapy."

She handed Lester and Anaïs a pair of headphones attached to a digital device. A neutral voice delivered an educational monologue:

"The orgone accumulator is a device designed by Dr Wilhelm Reich to collect, preserve, and intensify orgone energy. Orgone energy is cosmic life energy, the fundamental creative force long known to people in touch with nature, and speculated about by natural scientists, but now physically objectified and demonstrated. The orgone was discovered by Dr Reich, who identified many of its basic properties. For instance, orgone energy changes and radiates from all living and non-living substance. The properties of orgone energy derive from life itself, much in the manner of the older concepts of a vital force, or *elan vital*; unlike those older concepts, however, the orgone also has been found to exist in a mass-free form, in the atmosphere and in space. It is primary, primordial cosmic *life energy*, while all other forms of energy are secondary in nature...

"The interior surface of the accumulator is made of bare metal. The exterior surface is composed of orgone-absorbing, generally organic, non-metallic substance. An exceptionally powerful accumulator can be made using beeswax. The use of shellac has been proven not to disturb the flow of orgone energy, so that is what we have used here at the Orgone Institute.

"Although the shape of the accumulator is a factor of lesser importance than its material composition, machines in a conical or tetrahedron shape have yielded occasional life-negative effects. The best accumulators are therefore constructed in rectangular, cubical or cylindrical shapes. Accumulators are kept where fresh air can circulate. The door or lid should be kept partly open when not in use. Its interior may be kept fresh and sparkling by keeping an open basin of water sitting inside when not in use. Larger accumulators used by humans or farm animals are best kept outdoors in a sheltered area. Good air circulation and sunlight will assist with the accumulation effect. The accumulator will not develop a strong charge during wet, rainy weather. On such days, the orgone charge of the earth's surface is very low, most of it being taken up into the storm clouds overhead. The strongest charge is found on clear, sunny days, when the orgone charge at the earth's surface is also quite strong. Orgone accumulators used at higher altitudes tend to yield stronger charges. Do not use any household electrical appliances connected to a wall plug inside or near to the accumulator. Mobile phones and other radiating devices are strictly forbidden. When sitting inside, it is best to partially or completely disrobe, as heavy clothing will interfere with absorption of the orgone radiation."

They took their headphones off and handed them back. "Are you ready for your first session, sweetie?"

"I'm scared," Anaïs whispered.

"While she's here, I'll be able to come visit, won't I, doc?"

"Of course, Mr Langway."

"And I can talk to her on the phone?"

"We don't allow telephones around the orgone accumulators, but workers—we do not call them patients—can take and receive calls, most certainly."

Lester stroked her hair and kissed her on the cheek, nudged her towards the accumulator. She took her clothes off and handed them

My Week Without Gérard

to the smiling assistant who hung them on a peg for her. Inside the box, Anaïs sat on the wooden bench and gave Lester a brave-face smile. He never believed he could care for another human quite this much.

LVIII

On the way back to reception, Dr Reich explained how Anaïs would be inducted into "worker democracy". Residents who responded well to initial therapeutic activities participated in communal agriculture, trades such as carpentry and botany, reading groups, and musical performances.

"Don't believe the hype!" A screaming man was led away by a couple of men in lumberjack shirts. "They never metabolised potatoes here!"

"Arnold, we've told you before, the results were verified in scientific journals." Reich seemed to find the incident amusing, something he had to contend with every day, although he couldn't betray a sense of annoyance at these claims being made to an outsider.

"I'm a botanist, doc! I put a potato in the box! There was no correlation with lunar, solar or galactic parameters!" His voice echoed down the hall, and the sound of heels screeched on the floor.

The door to the ward—or rather, the "commune"—swung closed and locked behind them. "I hope that answers all your questions, Mr Langway."

Lester was dreading going back to Paris, or London, or anywhere that resembled conventional society. Even though he had his reservations about this place, he still felt compelled to ask, "Do you have room for one more?"

"I'm afraid we can't allow any previous relationships to influence the therapeutic process, at least at first. But if your girlfriend is here, and still wishes to see you in a month or two..."

"*Still wishes to see me*?!" He was starting to regret bringing her here again. "That patient, the botanist, what did he say about potatoes?"

"He's not a *patient*, he is a *worker*. And besides, he is a pathological liar. Is there anything else?"

"Pathological liar? Can you prove it? How do I know he's not telling the truth, and you're the pathological liar? Show me the scientific journals. I demand to see them."

The two beefy fellows in checked shirts appeared at his side, stinking of horse manure.

"Mr Langway, if you could sign yourself out of the guest book, we have a cab waiting for you outside."

He'd barely finished his squiggle when the two farm hands grabbed him and marched him out to the gravel, where a taxi with blacked-out windows was parked, revving its engine.

"There's such a thing as consent, you know!" Lester yelled over his shoulder. "If you touch her without her consent, I will destroy your reputation!"

Reich stood at the door of the institute, shrugging as if to say, "if only we had a reputation to destroy..."

The car doors locked. He was on his way back to hell.

LIX

Fedora hat tipped down over his face, drool pooled on the inner rim, Lester woke up at night on Rue Saint-Lazare. He staggered out of the cab and entered the door code. Up two flights of spiral stairs, he was aghast to discover that the party he'd heard from the street was happening on Mayakovsky's floor, perhaps even in his apartment. After the week he'd had, this was the last thing he needed. He opened the door to the Deadbeat Hotel expecting Mayakovsky and some vacuous fashion people snorting white powder, although the volume of electronic music should have warned him that something much more disturbing was happening. Even his most pessimistic visions could not have prepared him for the sheer volume of unwanted humanity he was about to encounter.

There must have been a hundred people at the party. The corridor was blocked by New Zealand meth peddlers in cut-off denims and models with shaved heads peering over the tops of one another like meerkats, pushing their way to the bathroom. A man in a New York Pet Rescue Service outfit charged through the crowd, accusing somebody of swiping his ferret.

Lester pushed into the dining room where twenty coked-up morons were screaming at one another about the Palestinian conflict. Some wealthy artworld floozy was playing a terrible version of an already unbearable Patti Smith song on guitar and getting irate when nobody except her cocaine buddy would listen.

Anything and anybody that impeded his ability to lie down and drift into unconsciousness was now an intolerable nuisance. Nothing, not even drugs or alcohol, had any intrinsic appeal. Still, with no chance of getting any sleep, Lester grabbed a bottle of Heineken, glugged it, and grabbed another, hoping it would make these humans slightly more tolerable. He wound up having—or rather, trying to get away from—a twenty-minute conversation with a wealthy furniture collector who was also a drug dealer, and wondered how much better an asylum would be.

Snow was offered and he took it off a key. He pushed through the crowds now with a new sense of urgency and a desire to fight or fuck somebody—possibly both. Undecoded libidinal messages were blasted into his cortex by the powder, so he pushed his way into the living room. Six fashion kids, strung out on some chemical, were occupying the coffin where he'd slept with Anaïs, and he realised how quickly time had moved, how nothing is permanent, and if that's the case, his reputation had been washed, and he ought to get back to being the cold-hearted bastard he always imagined himself to be. Strobe lights flashed from the bookshelves and industrial techno stretched his auditory canals—bang! bang! bang!—like cars being crushed.

As the female forms appeared in front of him, he realised, however, that while Anaïs was in the nuthouse, he was actually the one being held prisoner. He was, to borrow a phrase from Genet, a prisoner of love, screaming and yearning in the captivity of open space, whose vastness tormented him more than confinement. He had no emotional desire for any of the women in this room—they were all clearly far too stupid—but the very essence of their humanity reminded him of his suffering. These social whores were the clitoral nodes in a social system that had tormented and oppressed him, and their maintenance of that system had contributed, more than anything he had said or done, to the insanity of his lover, Anaïs, whose absence weighed on him like a ball and chain. He eyed up the jittery little buttocks in front of him twitching to Einstürzende Neubauten, and imagined penetrating them not out of love, but spite. Fucking them not because they reminded him of Anaïs—although something could be made of their superficial resemblance—but because they were *not* Anaïs. To fuck these girls would be a way of owning them, and owning them was the only way (besides murder) to knock them off the grid, erase them. As he saw it, each pussy he penetrated would effectively remove from his consciousness one being who was not Anaïs, and in doing so, increase the ratio of humanity that *was* Anaïs. Sure, he had preferences for whose vaginas he would like to penetrate among the crowd—preferring the young, skinny and androgynous to the old, hefty and overly smeared with makeup, for example—but when it came down to it, such choices were irrelevant. He had a singular ambition right now, and that was to reduce his suffering by increasing the amount of Anaïs in his world, and the only way he could envisage shrinking the world, and therefore his loneliness, was with a production-line gang bang.

Before he could thrust his crotch against the ripe young butt directly in front of him, however, a ripped, tanned drag queen took to the living room's makeshift stage and began fucking herself in the arse with something on a chain. Mayakovsky crouched down and clicked his camera—an anal action-shot. Gasps and cries as it turned out to be a ferret that had leapt out of the drag queen's arse and yanked itself off the finger. It ran around the room then, scattering the crowds with its chattering teeth and shit smell. A fat man in a string vest and gimp mask grabbed the ferret by the chain and whirled it round his head like a lasso, but a gaggle of anarchist vegan girls launched themselves at the twenty-stone ogre, pinning him against the wall and choking him. In the whirlpool of flesh, Lester crashed against the wall, his hat falling over his eyes again as the crowd's simultaneous gasps sucked all the oxygen from the air.

On closer inspection, it wasn't a drag queen who had been having sex with the ferret, but Rick Owens. Once the ferret's head had been spat out of the window, the fashion designer pulled his leather trousers up, wiped his bleeding arse and spoke into the microphone with a low California drawl. "Ladies and gentlemen, welcome to the Deadbeat Hotel. First of all, I would like to offer my condolences to Tim Sizebank, co-founder and editor of *Down N Out!* magazine, for the life-changing injury he sustained during a tragic accident earlier this week. And I would like to congratulate Susan Twanky on becoming the new editorial director of *Down N Out!* media, whose Parisian edition we are here to launch."

Drunken hollering, whistles and applause.

"Now I am going to describe some of my runway shows, which have been remixed into a poetry book, to be released in conjunction with *Down N Out!* media."

Whoops and cheers. "Go, Rick!"

"You're our Baudelaire!"

"Baudelaire? Dude, he's better than Shakespeare!"

"Luke, start the fucking music." *Cough cough.* "The women's fall/winter collection follows the men's fall/winter collection in being titled *Sisyphus* after the arrogant king in Greek mythology who was punished by Zeus to repeatedly roll a boulder up a hill only to have it roll back down again—eternally."

As ambient electronic music hissed from the speaker stacks, causing tension and excitement, Lester kept his eye on the girl in front, to see if her ass might be about to push backwards into his loins.

"We might interpret this as a story about futility, or as a story of patterns monotonously repeating themselves without progression."

But the sweat on the back of Lester's suit felt like a boulder. Bodies in leather and denim squashed against him from the side, pushing him further towards the coffin. The music rose in volume and tempo. The sound of marching boots layered into an electro cacophony. Strobe lights blared. Two models in army-style jackets with epaulets appeared onstage, saluting in rhythmic motions.

"The silhouette I fetishize this season is a high-waisted one with a rigid, almost military torso and a voluminous pelvis, the stiff drapery almost refuting sexuality with stately volume. 'Swans Reflecting Elephants' is the name of a Salvador Dali painting. But it's also a great feminized subtitle for this season's collection name, Mastodon. The women's collection continues this theme of evolution with soft abstractions folding around the body in a way that could reflect how we might one day calmly fold into the ether like in a Dali painting. I've always thought of runway shows as contemporary ceremonies. How can we use them in the most positive way? Deeply slit gowns in painted canvas or silk mega duchesse work over cashmere knit boxers and tanks. Shoes are stretch sock runners which are my version of an opera glove combined with a sneaker. The primordial splashes and drips that were more aggressive in the men's collection have been sweetened here in thick cupcake frosting. I've soundtracked this show to Beethoven's Piano Sonata No. 3 in C-Major—a great example of what civilization at its best sounds like."

Crushed against the door was a fellow in a bobble hat Lester recognised from his author photo. "Hey, you." In a sinister mood, he poked his rival in the chubby midrift.

"Yes? Hello?"

"Do you know who I am?"

"Umm." He was in his mid-thirties, obviously privately schooled, wearing skinny black jeans, an attempt to hide his obvious squareness. He pushed his designer geek-glasses up the bridge of his nose.

"You were sent to cover the Derenne story for *Down N Out!*, weren't you?"

"Yes!" Hugh Woolley seemed flattered by the recognition but also threatened. "Have we met before?"

The woman in her fifties Lester recognised from the British Press Awards—an event he had read about in the *Times*—interjected. "Wait, are you—"

Somebody burped in Lester's ear and spilled their drink over him. He steadied himself on the wall.

"—that Langway?!"

Vodka-coke in a plastic cup crushed against his cheek, and the impact sent him stumbling into a tall woman with grey hair smoking a thin cigarette. He grabbed her shoulders for balance and wound up staring her square in the face.

"Don't kiss me, you fucking creep. What are you doing here?"

"Sorry, I was pushed!"

Susan Twanky spat her cigarette out and singed his forehead with the ash. "Get the fuck away from me."

"I'm trying."

"Try harder. Security!"

She kicked him in the shin with the stiletto on her prosthetic leg. "Oww!" He tried to hop away, and as he did, two goons who looked like pitbull terriers yanked him into the air and were in the process of throwing him out of the window when a Mongolian throat singer and an Algerian beat boxer broke into Rick Owens' recital. Green lasers pierced the blood-scented smoke. Bodies gyrated, loosening the goons' grip on Lester, who was released into a swirl of black fabric. His hat was knocked off and landed back over his eyes. He wound up back in Wendy Woolley's vicinity. Luckily, she was out of drink to throw at him. Still, she lifted the fedora and looked him square in the eyes.

"Why are you still here?"

"This is the Deadbeat Hotel. I'm always welcome."

"Not anymore. You're a fucking creep. Leave us alone."

Hugh Woolley, with glasses steamed up, seemed to be high on ecstasy, as he jabbered into Lester's ear: "I loved your article about Ronnie O'Sullivan. Shame about the plagiarism!"

The crowd surged forward again. Groping forward, Lester accidentally latched onto Mrs Woolley's boob, and she swiped him across the face.

"He grabbed my breast! Susan! He assaulted me!"

"Wait," Lester pleaded. "Please, before I get ejected. Do you want Gérard's phone number? I've got it right here. Let me find it for you, then I'll leave, I promise."

Hugh and his mother looked at one another. They scrambled for their notebooks. "Darling, have you got your pen? Come on, write this down, it's important."

"Here, Hugh, pass me your notebook." Lester scrolled through his phone and wrote down Freddy's digits. "Good luck with the story. I hope one day you'll find it in your heart to forgive me."

Woolley and his mum were kissing one another on the lips when one of Twanky's goons lamped Lester on the side of the head. He dropped to the floor and tried to wriggle away. Crawling through fag butts, he found his feet by the mic stand. Rick Owens was jabbering in tongues over the guttural Mongolian/Algerian throat sounds, accompanied now by a midget with a harpsichord and a shaman casting spells.

Mayakovsky spotted him and tried to usher him to safety behind the DJ booth, but by that point Ridicula Goodman, who'd been in the front row the whole time, noticed who was swaying in the haze, and reacted as anyone who knew her expected she might. She leapt up and scissor-kicked him in the face. The force of her calves snapped his head back, and sent him crashing backwards into Rick Owens, who toppled out of the open window. The music stopped and shrill cries pierced the air. His models in the front row fought each other to get to the window and snap pictures of the Rick Owens corpse, swastickered on the pavement of Rue Saint-Lazare.

"Oh my god, Rick's dead!"

"No! What about the horse suicide?!"

"The poor horse!" they cried. "It won't get its five minutes with Rick!" While everybody rushed to the window, Ridicula Goodman took to the mic and announced: "It's Lester Langway! Don't let him get away! He assaulted me, and now he killed Rick Owens!"

"Patriarchal scum!"

"Psychopath!"

"Murderer!"

"Psychopathic, patriarchal scum!"

With spit raining down on him and kicks swinging into his midrift, Mayakovsky dragged Lester out the back entrance, locking the door behind them. On the fire escape, pinching his nose to keep the blood from spilling out, Lester said in a nasal voice: "Sorry for ruining your party, brother. I suppose I'm barred from the Deadbeat now?"

"No, of course not," Mayakovsky said. "You're always welcome."

"That's what all the dickheads were saying. They were calling for me to be deported to a prison colony."

"Were they? I'm not sure about that. I heard them calling you psychopathic, patriarchal scum, but there was no mention of a prison colony. How many fingers am I holding up?"

"Eight."

"I think you've got concussion. Here," Mayakovsky peeled his tshirt off. "Hold this to your face."

"Cheers," Lester tipped his head forward to stop the blood running down his throat. "Ouch!" He might have cracked a rib. "But didn't I just kill somebody?"

"Nah. Ridicula Goodman did."

"Alright, if you say so. Is he definitely dead?"

"Hmm, we'll see. One thing, though. You probably can't stay tonight."

"I don't want to stick around. They'll lynch me."

"Nah, they're fashion pussies. I could take them all down. But listen, where you need a cab to? Tell me where you want to go, I'll pay for it."

"Are you sure? There's no need..."

"Come on, you killed Rick."

"Wait, I thought you said Ridicula Goodman killed Rick."

"In my mind, you still get all the credit. If I sell the photos, I'm happy to split it with you."

"Are you sure?"

"Positive."

"Alright, it's a deal."

"So where do you want to go? I'm calling you a cab before the cops turn up."

"Hospital. Preferably the psych ward."

"Nah, there's nothing wrong with you, trust me. Name a bar."

"Alright. Le Tiki Lounge. I need a mai tai, urgently."

SUNDAY

LX

Having mixed fruity, rum-based cocktails with marijuana to the soothing sounds of Martin Denny until 4am with a pack of frozen raspberries pressed to his face, Lester didn't so much wake on the floor of Le Tiki Lounge as shine a light on his misery. Half a pint of blood must have dripped down his throat. Not that it really mattered. Mayakovsky had texted to reassure him that he wasn't wanted by the police in relation to Rick Owens' death, which ought to have made him happy. But all he could think about was Anaïs, and how she might never get out of the nuthouse. Considering the possibility that she wouldn't have wound up there if it wasn't for him, he wondered if perhaps she wasn't having paranoid delusions, but he really was the devil. Either way, the results were catastrophic. He had never felt so guilty or ashamed.

Waiting for the landlord, Cedric, to come and open the bar, he checked his phone to see if Anaïs had read any of his messages. Nope. When he woke from a few minutes of precious unconsciousness at 10am, he was elated to see her name finally flash up on the screen. Thank god they hadn't taken her phone away from her, and she could communicate with the outside world. There was hope.

"I'm not your babe," the message read. "I'm at the Orgone Institute now. Leave me alone."

He called, but she didn't answer. Dialled again, she cancelled the call. He ran behind the bar and poured himself a large glass of neat rum. With tears raining down his gashed and swollen face, he glugged and glugged, but the booze didn't even get him drunk. He ran to the toilet and vomited, wishing only that he had his packet of pills so that he could neck them all and finish himself off.

LXI

"My love for you is unconditional," he wrote in another text message. "Whatever you need from me, I'll do it. If you don't want to see me or hear from me ever again, it will break my heart, but I will accept it. Whatever you need. All I care about is your wellbeing."

He clutched the phone, shaking, threw himself on the floor and howled.

LXII

Anaïs was a master of brevity. "I love you too," she wrote. "Are you okay?"

"I feel better for hearing that. I still don't know where to go or what to do. Are you sure there's no room at the Institute for me?"

"You can't come here. Are you still in Paris?"

"Yes, but I can't stay here. Do you know anyone or anywhere I can go?"

She sent him a five-numbered postal code. "My friend will be there at midday. They're taking my phone off me now."

LXIII

Cedric came to let him out at eleven still wearing his tiki shirt, tossed his overnight guest a couple of strong painkillers and let him off the bill. He took a Métro to Gare du Lyon with a throbbing head and furry mouth, sharp pains when he breathed in, and the smell of himself so strong, it permeated a nose clotted with crusted blood. When he got there, Le Promenade café was opening to a bourgeois crowd ordering plates of greenery drizzled in balsamic vinegar. He took several coffees with shaking hands. By 12.50, when nobody had shown up to collect him, he started to wonder if Anaïs was playing tricks on him, and his bowels played up again.

In the bathroom, with thoughts of himself teetering over a precipice at Buttes Chaumont, he noticed a face on a poster. That couldn't have been the friend Anaïs mentioned, could it? He asked the waitress if she had the man's contact details. "Absolutely not," she said. "He reads tarot here on Wednesdays. Come back then and maybe you can speak to him."

He pleaded with her, and when that didn't work, he remembered enantiodromia: how systems inevitably become their opposites. Contrary to their reputation, the French were becoming the world's most servile creatures. All you have to do is wave some money at them, and their precious "liberté" goes down the drain.

So he peeled off his last ten-euro note and offered it to her. She snapped it out of his hand and wrote down an address.

LXIV

A few streets away in the east of Paris, Lester pressed a buzzer on an apartment building and stuttered: "Anaïs... schizophrenia... address... café... your book... a bomb... shelter... suicide... help." The door clicked open. Past the courtyard, he climbed the staircase with the sense that this might be the last one he ever ascended. If he was turned away now, he would either plead to be let in until the men in white coats came to take him away, or throw himself down the stairs.

He lost count of how many floors up it was in this distinctly unfussy building. He was getting dizzy when he came to a large set of double doors opened by a man who was shorter than he imagined—about his own height. His hair and beard were so white, they appeared to be made not out of human hair, but the tips of duck feathers. He wore an expression of worldly calm and concern, as though many people had flocked to him over the years in desperate need of his special guidance.

Lester didn't know what to say, so threw himself into the great man's arms and embraced him. "You have saved my life!"

LXV

That special Sunday morning light shone through the window of the cosy atelier. Lying on the sofa, he could smell a bagel toasting. The kindly old gentleman was pottering around in a patchwork bathrobe, watering his plants. His bookshelves contained all the major religious works, plus more obscure titles in eastern and esoteric traditions. One wall had a huge framed poster of *The Holy Mountain*, one of Lester's favourite films. On the coffee table was a hardback copy of *Dune*, a storyboard for the film that was never made—one of only two copies in existence. When the old man handed Lester the smoked salmon and cream cheese bagel, he rubbed his eyes. Yes, it was really him.

He told Lester about the Japanese belief that if you save somebody's life, you have a duty to help them.

"No you don't, you really don't." With a pack of frozen peas pressed against his head, Lester told him about the amazing coincidence that brought them together. In her befuddled state, Anaïs had sent him to the wrong address—the postal code was one digit out—and so he had ended up at the café where Alejandro Jodorowsky read tarot.

"What a remarkable coincidence! But you should understand, I never looked to earn my living through the cards. However, I wanted to, at one time, study the tarot further. So I went to Rue des Lomards to the bookstore called Arcane 22 that specialises in the tarot. Because the owners respected me, I suggested that they outfit a little room in the rear of the boutique and hire me to receive two people per day for six months to give professional readings. They posted an ad, and clients came. I am not going to exaggerate my idea of the tarot. Suffice it to say, I do not read the future but I contend myself with the present and focus the client on self knowledge, starting from the principle that it is useless to know the future if one ignores who one is here in the moment."

"I've spent too long trying to forget who I am," Lester said.

"To enter into a person's difficulties is to enter into his family, to penetrate the psychological atmosphere of his domestic milieu. We are all marked, not to say contaminated, by the psychomental universe of our people. A number of people have associated with them a personality that is not theirs, one that is borrowed from one or more members of their emotional environment. To be born into a family is to be, if I may say it this way, possessed."

"Anaïs says she was possessed by me, and that I am the devil."

"That's entirely plausible, but we'll come to that a little later," Jodorowsky said. "Possession usually is transmitted from generation to generation. The enchanted becomes the enchanter in projecting onto his children what was projected onto him—unless an awakening comes to break the cycle. To undo a difficulty, it is not enough to clearly identify the problem. An awakening that is not followed by action serves nothing. From that, little by little, I glimpsed that I had to advise people. For the awakening to become operable, I must make the person act, lead them to commit a very precise act. Thus, the birth of the psychomagic act."

It was strange hearing Jodorowsky talk about the work in the book that had been blown to pieces outside the bookshop. Almost like he was living in one of an infinite number of alternate realities, where that event had never taken place.

"Soon I will prescribe you a psychomagical act. It will be irrational in appearance, but rational in that you will know why it needs to be done. I should warn you that all psychomagic acts have perverse—that is to say, uncontrollable—effects. Which is precisely what gives psychomagic its richness."

"Will it cost me anything?"

"To perform psychomagic is to enter into a contract not only with me, but with the cosmic forces in the universe. I do not accept financial payments, although you must proceed with extreme caution before entering into this pact. It comes with a stipulation that makes it one of the most significant—and perhaps, costly—decisions you will ever make."

"I'm ready for it."

"In order for the solution to your life's problems to be effective, you must agree to complete the act, in its entirety, *before* I prescribe it to you, and therefore before you know what it will be. I must warn you in advance that the psychomagic act could be anything! It could be relatively simple and straightforward, and take only a few minutes, or it could require your undivided attention for months. The psychomagic act could be beautiful and bizarre, or it could be relatively unremarkable. Should you agree to take on the psychomagic act, you may be required to do something that society regards as immoral or disgusting, even illegal. It might frighten you, repulse you, or take you beyond the pain threshold. It may cause you to lose friends or worse.

"The second condition of the psychomagic act is that you must not tell another human soul, besides myself, what you are doing or why you are doing it.

"Third, and finally, when you have completed the act, you must write me a letter describing in detail how you did it, with evidence that you have completed it. This is the only payment I ask. If you lie to me, or you do not complete the act within one year, I will know about it, and you will be killed. Think about it carefully for a few moments before you tell me if you wish to proceed."

Lester finished his tea. He was both scared and reassured by the epic, poetic nature of Jodorowsky's presence. It must have meant that he was the real deal.

"The psychomagic act could be absolutely *anything*?" Lester clarified.

"Anything within the realm of human possibility!"

"Even fucking my own mother?"

"Perhaps!"

Lester downed his tea and asked if he could smoke on the balcony. Alejandro obliged.

LXVI

Outside, watching the cars go by on the boulevard beneath him, that endless flow of banality, Lester ran through his life's options and problems, his quest for something more than the average, and concluded that the only way he could lose would be by turning down Jodorowsky's offer.

He kicked his boots off and joined Jodorowsky at the dining room table, where the guru was laying out a tarot deck. "Jodo, I have decided."

"Yes?"

"I'm going to perform the psychomagic act."

"Of course you are. I knew that before you went outside. But still, it's good to think things over, acquaint yourself with what might be the last way of ever thinking and behaving in this manner."

"Oh goody." Lester rubbed his hands together, imagining a future in which he was as wise and at one with the universe as Jodorowsky. "I'm excited."

"Before taking on a client, it is important that I acquire a perfect knowledge of you. Since people only tend to make partial confessions, I will start with a tarot reading to expose certain shameful secrets right off the bat."

He spread the cards across the table and shuffled them with his paper-like hands, over and under one another, until they were regulated like the feathers on a bird of prey.

"To choose a card is to tear a hole in the conscious, and see into the unconscious. Hover your hands over the cards, and when you feel the attraction of a certain card, pick it up and turn it over."

Lester closed his eyes and felt a magnetic pull emanating from below his right hand. He reached down and flipped the card over.

"Oh my, oh my," Jodorowsky said. "You have chosen Le Monde, Arcanum 21, the card with the highest numerical value." Even though he had given thousands of readings, Jodorowsky had not lost his sense of wonder at what the cards—and therefore the universe—could turn over.

"Because it has been placed as the final point and in the position of fulfilment, The World indicates a major realisation. It is an accomplished woman, a soul in full joy, a perfect world, a happy marriage, worldly success."

He spoke in a jarringly melancholy register.

"This card can also inspire travel: the discovery of the world in the literal sense of the term. Just as Arcanum 16, The Tower, can evoke a male penis in the process of ejaculating, Arcanum 21 brings to mind a female sex organ inhabited by an exultation (orgasm) or an individual (pregnant woman)."

On their two attempts, Lester was pretty sure he hadn't impregnated Anaïs. But still, he didn't want children, so now he suspected why Jodorowsky seemed downbeat.

"On the other hand, if the card appears at the beginning of the reading, it represents a difficult beginning: the card is not in its rightful place and becomes an imprisonment. The realisation is demanded before any action. We must now look for traces of the first traumatising experience which has therefore formed an obstacle to your development. So I am going to ask you a series of questions about yourself, from your grandparents to your present relationships, and I demand that you answer me truthfully, so that I can prescribe the appropriate psychomagic act."

Jodorowksy spent the next couple of hours quizzing Lester, probing into the dark corners of his personality.

LXVII

"To prescribe a psychomagic act is to enter directly into the language of the unconscious," Jodorowsky said finally, as a judge might sum up a case. "From what you have told me, and what the cards have revealed, you are a mental and moral weakling, an extremely profane young man with a drug and alcohol problem, and you have a fear of inferiority that stems from your upbringing."

Out of respect, Lester tried to maintain eye contact with a man who was so obviously his superior. His eyes twitched, and he plugged them with his fingers as his conscious mind resisted the painful truths to which it was being exposed.

"When I consider these facts in conjunction with your tarot card, symbolising a total realisation, I come to the conclusion that you must perform a symbolic act that addresses the fundamentals of your existence, your sexuality and your relationship with your parents."

"What is it?" Lester asked, quivering.

After a long pause, Jodorowsky whispered something in Lester's ear.

The young man's eyes widened as the magic prescription hit his brain. It was going to feel very, very strange, Jodorowsky warned, to do something that was so contrary to his instincts. But as soon as he had completed it, he would have realigned his position with the universe, and he would feel, for the first time, like he truly belonged in it.

"Don't worry, you don't have to do it now. You have a year to complete the act," Jodorowsky reassured him. "Since I feel somewhat responsible for you, take some money to make sure you get home."

Ordinarily, Lester would have refused the offer out of pride, but he knew that Jodorowsky didn't do anything that was not perfectly harmonious with nature. He took the notes and stuffed them in his wallet.

"And another thing. Don't forget to take the tarot card with you. I have a feeling it might open a door or two for you."

LXVIII

In a cab on his way out of Paris, another text message from Anaïs: "You'll never guess who I met here."

"No, who?"

"I was telling her about my boyfriend..."

He felt so good to hear that word, *boyfriend*.

"Please..."

"She says you were wasted when you met her. It seems to be a common theme."

"Hey, stop needling me. I've had enough trauma for one week."

"Janice Remarque. Remember her?"

Gulp. "You're joking?"

"No. I don't make jokes anymore. This place isn't funny."

"Are you okay?"

"She says they brought her here against her will."

"Who's *they*?"

"She says you'll know what she means."

"You're not implying that I did that, are you?"

"No. But she wants her night-vision goggles back."

"Alright, I took them by mistake. Why is she there?"

"She was diagnosed with schizophrenia. Just like me!"

"Oh shit. Are you safe?"

"I think so. It's just weird here."

"Do you want to leave?"

"Yes. We both want to leave."

"Can you wait until tomorrow?"

"Yes."

"Alright, let me finish this job, then I'll be with you."

LXIX

"Step on it!" Lester handed the driver a fifty-euro note flecked with speed and bloody bogeys.

The target emerged from his apartment in a retirement village-style complex in Neuilly at 3pm and got into a Mini Cooper. Lester presumed the bag he'd thrown into the boot was his swimming kit. "Follow that man. I'll pay you whatever it costs."

Taking the western route around the city, they missed the running battles that had spread from the 1st Arrondisement to the outer districts, where theatres, art galleries and other cultural institutions were being attacked by angry mobs. An hour later, they stopped at a service station. Lester was tempted to get out and accompany his man to the urinal, eavesdrop on a phone conversation, perhaps, but he stayed in the car icing the cuts and bruises on his face.

Later, with the sun going down above the sunflower fields in the Burgundy region and the holiday song 'Route Nationale Sept' by Charles Tenet on the radio, Lester slumped in the back seat with his feet up, laughing at updates from Freddy, who had coaxed Hugh and Wendy Woolley to drive a hundred miles in the opposite direction towards Calais. In flashes of sunlight through Napoleonic trees, he thought about the arc of his narrative so far and how, like Breton, he too had no use for the "empty moments" in his life. But as soon as this hectic week was over, he would assure his detractors that he didn't give a damn about any of this and repeat:

Leave everything.
Leave Dada.
Leave your wife, leave your mistress.
Leave your hopes and fears.
Drop your kids in the middle of nowhere.
Leave the substance for the shadow.
Leave behind, if need be, your comfortable life and promising future.
Take to the highways.

My Week Without Gérard

The target slowed down at a police roadblock outside the village of Saint-Benin d'Anzy. The only residents appeared to be scraggly cats, an Englishman walking a blind dog and humble, rural folk. Lester told the driver to keep his distance from the car in front. But the driver had already got out of his Mini and was gesturing in their direction to a cop, who waited for the host of *Paris Culture* to drive through the barrier before waving them forward.

"Papers, please?" The cop squinted at Lester's passport. "What's an Englishman doing in a Paris taxi all the way out here?"

"I'm going to a party."

"Do you have the address?"

"It's a special kind of party. We'll receive the address this evening."

The officer must have been instructed to delay them until the Mini Cooper was out of sight. Now that it was, they were allowed to pass.

But they caught up with the famous TV host as he was pulling through the gates of a white chateau set back from the road, with turrets and paddocks for horses, a walled garden. It was a residence that once belonged to the local duke.

Lester got out and approached the gate, taking deep breaths. He pressed the buzzer and waited, looking into the camera, projected the image of himself as a no-shit-taken kind of guy.

"Hello," a familiar scowling voice. "What do you want?"

"Remember me? I've come to return your book."

After a couple of seconds, Lester flashed him first the Breton biography, then The Hanged Man tarot card.

"You'd better come in."

The gate slid open and Lester pumped his fist. Jodorowsky really was a magician.

Walking up the long, sunny driveway, Lester could see the chateau doors were already open. It was like a fancy bed and breakfast. There were no women in eyepatches or other strange uniforms, no security guards. An atrium branched off into a large rustic kitchen and a dining room, with a 17th Century chapel adjoined to the eastern side. His heart sprang with joy when he detected a whiff of chlorine from what he assumed was a swimming pool at the western wing.

A man who resembled Gérard Derenne entered the hallway in a dressing gown, "GD" initials embroidered on the breast pocket in a gold flourish script. He was only a couple of inches taller than Lester in his slippers, and he smelled of aftershave. The hair that tumbled over his shoulders was totally grey now. His nose was more hooked than in photos, with a strange flatness to the tip that was normally disguised by makeup. The skin around his eyes sagged and the charisma in them had faded. His right hand was bandaged, so he didn't offer it to shake.

"Mr Langway?"

"Gérard Derenne?"

"No, we are always mistaken for one another. I am his twin brother, Marc. Julien says you followed him all the way from Paris. We are declining guests at the moment, but I said to Julien, I think we should make an exception for this chap, he's shown dedication, and we must be hospitable to our English cousins. We have put the kettle on for you. How do you like your tea?"

"Milk, two sugars, please."

"Okay, I'll have Jacques make it for you. Come this way. We're watching television."

In the living room, Badbeger was in a comfy chair with a folded copy of the Sunday paper on his lap. An old TV was on, showing the scenes outside Théâtre du Châtelet. The cops had blocked the doors and were putting the boot into the few rioters remaining outside, but the mob had managed to secure the building. The anchor couldn't confirm it, but there were reports that the audience and actors were being terrorised and assaulted.

Then a rough-looking skinhead with a bloodied face appeared alongside the interviewer. "Well, it is a sad fact that organisations base their success on deception," he said. "This should be self-evident, but is generally overlooked due to the moral codes elitists foist on their subjects."

"Maybe you could furnish us with a few examples?"

"Visible leaders make themselves vulnerable. By embracing deception, we believe our Leader has fashioned the ultimate system yet devised for the secure exercise of power."

The other men behind him, many of whom were hooded in black, nodded in formal appreciation of his knowledge.

"Are you coming from the right or the left?" the interviewer asked.

"The Right and Left will never join forces to overturn a monopolistic system," he said. "While the elite, completely free of prejudice, supports both sides and none, in this battle for its own ends."

The men in cloaks and hoods jumped the news anchor. They tackled the cameraman, whose vantage was now the ground. Hooded and bloodied faces loomed over the screen, which still projected behind them, skewed and out of focus, the image of Gérard, with flares going off all around him, on the theatre behind them.

"Power moved from the priesthood to the kings to the bourgeoisie, until now it resides in the mob!"

"Reality has fragmented into segments you can travel through, like dreams!"

"Immanentize the eschaton!"

"Immanentize the eschaton!"

"IMMANENTIZE THE ESCHATON!"

Badbeger looked over his shoulder at Lester and then away again, as though they had never met. He shook his head, zapped the TV off with the remote. "Why don't you give the professor his book back and leave us alone?"

Jacques Dutronc had an ironing board set up by the window and was running the iron over one of Derenne's shirts while puffing on a cigarillo.

"Pardon me," Derenne bellowed at Dutronc. "Would you mind not smoking over our shirts?!"

Dutronc muttered something under his breath about watching the news and stubbed his fag out. "I apologise for shouting. He's becoming deaf as a doornail. Jacques! Go and make the young man a cup of tea! The kettle's boiled! Mr Langway, how did you say you like it?"

"It's really not a problem, I'm fine. Don't on account of me, please, professor."

"Alright, then. But only if you insist, Mr Langway. It's really no problem for us, we love our tea in this house, don't we, Jacques?"

Lester cocked his head at Dutronc, his grey hair stack, those beady eyes and Adam's apple bobbing. "So he is your... housekeeper? I assumed you would have a maid."

"No, Mr Langway. Jacques travels everywhere with Gérard. Always has, always will. He is one of the world's leading authorities on Immanuel Kant, you know. Allow me to demonstrate how he is the living, breathing conscience of this organisation. He is the physical manifestation of the categorical imperative..."

"The moral law. But I was going to say, those scenes in Paris..."

"You've read your Kant," Derenne smiled, a tad condescendingly. He was clearly used to speaking in monologues rather than having two-way conversations. "Well done. In that case, let me show you around. This place used to belong to Colonel Rémy, the great resistance leader who became one of our mentors and dear friends. Lord Balthazar, the fudge magnate, lived here briefly in the 1980s. Then it was bought by Johnny Hallyday, a very good friend of ours who has generously leant it to Gérard."

Lester tried to interject, but Derenne cantered through conversation like an Olympic dressage horse.

"Johnny built the recording studio in the garden, where some of the most famous French musicians have recorded, such as Sasha Distel, another close family friend. This is where he and Johnny made Gérard's album, *Monsieur Amour*."

"A classic. I was listening to it at—nevermind, continue."

"Of course, we attract pilgrims, rubber neckers, journalists. They ring the bell and ask if they can come in and take photographs of the swimming pool where Roman Polanski was said to have made love to a swan. Gérard told dear old Jacques that nobody is to enter the grounds of this house under *any circumstances* if Gérard is not here. Even if Jesus Christ himself were to arrive unannounced, he must be turned away. But would you believe, on the evening we moved our belongings into the house—after a brief disagreement over who would cook the veal and who would do the washing-up that night—Gérard told Jacques that he was going for a walk. But the cloth-eared old devil mustn't have heard him, because Gérard left without taking his key, and of course when he returned many hours later, fatigued and thirsty, like Jesus after dragging that cross up a hill—for he had been strenuously *thinking* all that time—he pressed the buzzer and dear old Jacques wouldn't let him in. Gérard pleaded with him through the intercom. At first Gérard thought he had trouble hearing, but he heard alright. 'Gérard, you told me not to let anybody in while you were away, and I promised that's what I would do,' he said. To his credit, Gérard called him all the names under the sun. Didn't he, dearest Jacques? But he wouldn't go back on his promise, saying it would be an abdication of his duty. They had a raging argument about the flaws in Kant's moral law. Gérard even quoted at length from his own book on the subject, but Jacques was as stubborn as a billy goat. For two hours they yelled at each other through the intercom. Jacques kept insisting that he *was* serving the ultimate good, because it would teach Gérard to be more precise with his instructions. Eventually, Gérard decided the only choice would be to get help from one of our neighbours. Gérard explained to Monsieur Muron, a humble cattle farmer, that he was dealing with a Kantian of the highest order, who would rather go to his grave than let him into his own house. They're not anarchists out here, they respect property. But the farmer suggested that they ram the gates with a tractor. This they did, and Gérard had to knock Jacques unconscious with his bare fists as he guarded the door with a kitchen knife."

Derenne put his arm around Dutronc's shoulder as he sprayed starch onto the shirts. "Look here," he twisted his head towards his guest and pointed to the cut above his eye. "Six stitches."

"Interesting," Lester said. "And Monsieur Derenne, what happened to your hand?"

"Grrrr!" Dutronc snapped and Derenne jumped away from him, shaking his fingers.

"The soldier! Ask him about the soldier who came here!"

At that interjection, Badbeger darted across the room and rugby tackled Dutronc, knocking over the ironing board and scalding them both. Julien gagged the old Kantian philosopher with a sock, but it was too late—a truth had been revealed.

With Dutronc now muzzled, Derenne sat back in an armchair with his balls dangling out, whirling his wrist in the air, as if letting go of a cord to the light he had just turned on. "So there you go, that explains everything, does it not?"

EPILOGUE

I

I sought a theme and sought for it in vain,
I sought it daily for six weeks or so.
Maybe at last being but a broken man
I must be satisfied with my heart, although
Winter and summer till old age began
My circus animals were all on show,
Those stilted boys, that burnished chariot,
Lion and woman and the Lord knows what.

II

What can I but enumerate old themes,
First that sea-rider Oisin led by the nose
Through three enchanted islands, allegorical dreams,
Vain gaiety, vain battle, vain repose,
Themes of the embittered heart, or so it seems,
That might adorn old songs or courtly shows;
But what cared I that set him on to ride,
I, starved for the bosom of his fairy bride.

And then a counter-truth filled out its play,
'The Countess Cathleen' was the name I gave it,
She, pity-crazed, had given her soul away
But masterful Heaven had intervened to save it.
I thought my dear must her own soul destroy
So did fanaticism and hate enslave it,
And this brought forth a dream and soon enough
This dream itself had all my thought and love.

And when the Fool and Blind Man stole the bread
Cuchulain fought the ungovernable sea;
Heart mysteries there, and yet when all is said
It was the dream itself enchanted me:
Character isolated by a deed
To engross the present and dominate memory.
Players and painted stage took all my love
And not those things that they were emblems of.

III

Those masterful images because complete
Grew in pure mind but out of what began?
A mound of refuse or the sweepings of a street,
Old kettles, old bottles, and a broken can,
Old iron, old bones, old rags, that raving slut
Who keeps the till. Now that my ladder's gone
I must lie down where all the ladders start
In the foul rag and bone shop of the heart.

—William Butler Yeats, 'The Circus Animals' Desertion'

FEATURING

Mark Polizzotti, *Revolution of the Mind: The Life of André Breton* (1995)

André Breton, *The First Manifesto of Surrealism* (1924)

André Breton, *The Second Manifesto of Surrealism* (1929)

André Breton & Philippe Soupault, *The Magnetic Fields* (1920)

André Breton, *Nadja* (1928)

Georges Simenon, *Maigret's First Case* (1948)

Georges Simenon, *Maigret's Mistake* (1953)

Georges Simenon, *Inspector Cadaver* (1944)

Raymond Queneau, *Zazie dans le Métro* (1959)

Georges Bataille, *Blue of Noon* (1957)

RD Laing, *The Divided Self* (1960)

Alejandro Jodorowsky, *Psychomagic* (2010)

Antonin Artaud, *The Theatre, Its Double* (1938)

Nikolas and Zeena Schreck, *Demons of the Flesh: The Complete Guide to Left Hand Path Sex Magic* (2002)

Peter Haining (ed.) *The Necromancers: The Best of Black Magic and Witchcraft* (1971)

Carl Jung, *Synchronicity* (1952) & other works

Jade Lingard & Xavier de la Porte, *The Impostor* (2011)

Colin Wilson, *The Occult* (1971)

Rodney Orpheus, *The Grimoires of Aleister Crowley* (2019)

Peter Levenda, *Sinister Forces: The Nines, Vol. 1* (2011)

Patrick Lepetit (trans. Jon E Graham), *The Esoteric Secrets of Surrealism* (2014)

Wilhelm Reich, *The Discovery of the Orgone* (1961)

James Meo, PhD. And Eva Reich, MD., *The Orgone Accumulator Handbook* (1989)

Anonymous, *The Occult Technology of Power: The Inititation of the Son of a Finance Capitalist into The Arcane Secrets of Economic and Political Power* (1974)

Guy Debord, *Society of the Spectacle* (1967)

Tobias Churton, *Occult Paris* (2016)

Andrew Marr, *My Trade* (2004)

Alain Robbe-Grillet & Alain Resnais (dir.), *Last Year at Marienbad* (1961)

Jean-Pierre Melville (dir.), *Le Samouraï* (1967)

Jean-Luc Godard (dir.), *Breathless* (1961)

Marcel Carné (dir.), *Hotel du Nord* (1938)

Tristan Tzara, 'To Make a Dadaist Poem' (1920)

William Butler Yeats, 'A Vision' (1925)

William Butler Yeats, 'The Circus Animals' Desertion' (1939)

Rick Owens, Press Releases (2010—)

MUSIC

Serge Gainsbourg, 'Intoxicated Man' (1962)

Magali Noël, 'Strip-Rock' (1956)

Charles Aznavour, 'Le Feutre Taupé' (1956)

Catherine Sauvage, 'Black Trombone' (1962)

Françoise Hardy, 'Tous le Garçons et Les Filles' (1962)

Claude Nougaro, 'Le Cinéma' (1962)

Alain Goraguer, 'C'est Mortel Ennuie' (1959)

Nino Ferrer, 'Looking for You' (1974)

Charles Trenet, 'Route National Sept' (1959)

Johnny Hallyday, 'Noir C'est Noir' (1966)

Erik Satie, 'Gnossienne #1' (1889)

Claude Debussy, 'Arabesque' (1888)